FLOWERS FOR ADAM

BY JOHNNY WRAITH

FLOWERS FOR ADAM

First Edition July 2010

Written by Johnny Wraith

The stories Johnny Wraith writes are fiction.
All characters and places and events are imaginary.

ISBN 978-0-557-56913-7

Copyright © 2010 by Johnny Wraith
All rights reserved

Contact Johnny Wraith at: www.johnnywraith.com

To you, so you don't waste another minute
– this fleeting life might be all you ever get

Chapter 1 – Tumble off the bridge and into the water

Nothing happens for a reason or according to any one's plan, whether you are a man, woman, beast, demon, or deity, planet, plant or a stone. Everything is just a small step or a wiggle in a perfectly choreographed, absurdly chaotic dance with no origin or cause, or purpose. There is no good or evil, or real time, or true folly or hardship or abundance or dearth, loss or gain, but only the moment's laughter and tears, food and drink, sex and bowel movements, spastic orgasms, searing pain, obsession, addiction, ejaculation, spitting, bleeding, decay, searing pain, anxiety, fear, conquest, surrender, love, hate, failure and victory, the strokes of a paintbrush or of a pen, a glimmer of hope, the sudden loss of it all, and in no particular order, birth and death with countless slumbers and awakenings in between, rebirth and re-death. We can't ever grasp it, but sometimes we might catch its colors or sounds, or the tastes or palpability of it, as she whisks through our hair and over our skin with her invisible fingers, but only when we are looking the other way.

You must blindly leap into the darkness to chase after fireflies, but don't try to catch them. Go from one to the next, to the next. Never put them in jars.

One day, I stumbled off a bridge and into the water.

Chapter 2 – The fish

Before I tell you how I tumbled off a bridge and into the water, I must tell you how I ended up on that bridge in the first place. It all began with debauchery, the kind involving my concurrent consumption of Absinthe and shrooms, and a few other things, while vacationing in Amsterdam. I was searching my soul.

But really, you might ask, why ingest Absinthe and shrooms? Couldn't you have searched your soul in other ways? Perhaps, but that's not the way it happened. There is no reason to question why I consumed what I consumed at this point. It is too late to puke it back up. Now we are stuck only with why I was searching my soul. In short, I was lost, decadent, irresponsible, a criminal, dissatisfied, depressed, enduring a mid-life crisis, and otherwise trying to compensate for personal failings. But then again, none of this matters now, even if it did matter then.

Why?

Because I am now in a different place and I am telling you my story for your sake, not mine. Do not be concerned with me or why I do or did the things I do, or did. The journey you are about to take, by looking through my eyes, is your journey, not mine, though it was my journey and now it is your journey. I'm no longer a part of it. You are now the protagonist. Not me. Enjoy this story as *you* live it, for it is one of folly and adventure, but most importantly, it is a form of personal instruction. This story is for you and it is about you. Besides, you may never know me but through these words, whether they are reaching your eyes from your computer screen, a book, or a pamphlet. I am irrelevant, and you are everything. I am no thing.

Nevertheless, there I was in Amsterdam, searching, playing hide and go seek with things that can only be found by first altering the mind and spirit. Perhaps I would find enlightenment. Did I? Once again, this is for you to decide. Keep reading. Even if I didn't find it, maybe you will.

The morning after my arrival, in Amsterdam, I had an omelet and a triple espresso for breakfast, and then began touring the city on foot. I saw the Anne Frank House, visited Vincent van Gogh paintings in the art museums, and strolled along the Red Light District so I could peek in the windows at the girls for sale. Cheap thrills! On numerous occasions in-between, I found myself sitting on various barstools throughout the city, doing shot after shot of Absinthe. By suppertime I was drunk, stumbling over cracks in the cobblestone streets, and apologizing each time I lost my balance and tripped into a tourist.

"Watch it buddy!"

"Bastaard!"

Perhaps the hashish lollypops I'd purchased from a vendor just outside the Anne Frank House caused some of the trouble; they may have contributed to my vomiting into a public trashcan.

"Bleeeeeccccchhhhhhh!"

"Jezus!"

It was funny how even in Amsterdam, a city tolerant of drug experimentation and hallucinogenic alcohol, hash suckers, sex shows, and hookers, you still received sneers and rude comments from passers-by while heaving up sickness. The worst of it wasn't the bad publicity. It was that even after I had partaken of enough drink and marijuana candy to puke headfirst into a public trashcan for an audience of squeamish tourists, I still wasn't hallucinating. Instead, I was only half awake, slouching on a bench (next to a trashcan filled with my barf), barely able to stand or walk, and my mouth tasted like rotting vomit. But, as I was sitting there (slouching) pondering whether to give up or keep going, whether I would be coherent enough to find the train back to my hotel, let alone the train station, I realized I was sitting across from a small pizza parlor. By cupping one hand over an eye to offset my double vision, I was able to read the sidewalk menu board. The special of the day was:

Cheese Pizza with Shrooms = $10.5 E

I think it was frozen pizza and the place didn't serve any booze other than wine and beer, but the meal wasn't too bad. The tomato sauce was sweet and the little white diced mushrooms abundantly sprinkled on top of the pie were raw and strangely bitter. I ate the whole pizza and washed it down with a carafe of house wine. Paid the bill, and got out of there. Disappointed I was still only feeling drunk after such a promising meal, I decided to stumble my way back to the train station, get back to the hotel and get some sleep. Maybe I'd have a few unusual dreams. It wasn't an easy task – walking that is. With every step I had to fight for my balance, and a few times I tripped over a raised cobblestone and fell. After a couple falls, my skinned knees were bleeding through my jeans, but luckily I didn't hit my head or break any bones. On my way, I crossed over many bridges. Amsterdam is a city with many canals, and bridges.

Each time I crossed over one of the many bridges, I heard someone calling my name, as if it were coming from below.

"Johnny! Johnny!"

Was I imagining things? Maybe the shrooms were starting to work?

"Johnny! Johnny!"

No, it can't be.

"Johnny! Johnny!" squealed the high-pitched voice, even louder than before. If my ears weren't fooling me, it was coming from below, from near the water, between the abutments. I stopped in the middle of the bridge, cupped my hand to my ear, and listened.

"Johnny! Johnny! Come over to the railing and look down. I'm down here! In the water!"

I stumbled over to the railing, leaned over and looked down. An orange fish with a human face was looking up out of the water at me. It was about the size of a cat.

"What the... ...!" I spoke aloud.

"What the... ...!" replied the fish. "What is a fish? I am a talking fish. You may have never met a talking fish, but you have never had pizza with magic mushrooms before, have you?"

"Well, no. You do have a point there. I'm Johnny, by the way."

"I know your name, you idiot! How else was I calling you by it? Think before you speak, why don't you?"

I was finally starting to enjoy myself. The shrooms were working! This is going to become a great story, I thought to myself. Just go with the flow, talk to the fish. See what happens next. Of course, I was imagining things. I knew that much. I was having a vivid dream while still awake. A blessing brought on by medicinal fungus. A good cheese pizza.

"My name is Vatsulu," declared the fish, as it rose up out of the water on a fluttering tail and proudly flapped its fins. "I was once a human, like you, and I've been a number of other things. I've been a flower, a bear, an insect, a dog, and a cat, not to mention a number of other things, perhaps a thousand or a million. I am to be your animal guide."

"Who told you to guide me?"

"No one. We simply crossed paths when you were in tune with the other world. In fact, we spoke yesterday. That's when we had our formal introduction."

"I didn't talk to you yesterday. I would have remembered that."

"We did talk. Or at least I spoke to one of your other selves. He was running about a day ahead of you, at this very bridge. I don't expect you to understand because you think in terms of time, as if things really happen in a particular order, and things don't really happen in any particular order. Nothing is linear. You'll never fully grasp what I'm saying in this life, but to make a long story short, as a flesh and blood being you live in a realm with only one dimension. All you've ever known is a flat world when the real world is round and full of many curves."

"Real world?"

"Call it the other world if you wish, though that's really where you are from my perspective. Where you are it's just too flat and boring. Where I am there are lots of curves!"

"Vatsulu, if I've ever seen a curve, I think I'm seeing one now."

"Quite the contrary, my friend. You are not *seeing* a curve. You can't see such things with your eyeballs. You are *feeling* the curve, from your gut."

"But I am *seeing* a talking fish."

"No, you really aren't *seeing* me. You aren't *hearing* me either."

"So I am imagining things?"

"Yes and no. No, because there is more to it than imagining, as you typically define it. Yes, because you are imagining something real. Usually your mind imagines things that don't really exist, but when you are really tuned in, as you are now, you can imagine real things. That's the only way to do it because your senses are too dull to see, hear, touch, taste, or smell my world or any thing in it. Only because you are filled with magic are you able to sense a higher reality, its chaos, splendor, randomness, its curvature and answerless puzzles and conundrums. Still, you are like a blind man feeling your way through a place brightly painted in rainbow colors and adorned in silver and gold."

"Vatsulu?"

"Yes?"

"You are full of a beautiful abundance of shit, and I like it."

"Are you ready to join me on an adventure you'll never forget?" With this loaded question, Vatsulu winked at me and smiled, and then he playfully swirled about on his tail, flapping his fins and splashing the water.

"How do I join you? You're a fish. Unless you can sprout legs and come out of the water?"

"Quite the contrary, my friend. You are going to sprout fins, a tail, and gills, so you can join me in the water. After all, there is a lot more water than land, and in water you can swim in any direction. Up, down, upside down and sideways. You can ride the currents wherever they go. On land you can only go one way, and that is straight. You are too heavy and wingless to follow the wind out there. Just jump in! Time is being wasted, to put it metaphorically, because after all, there is no such thing at time."

This was the part of the shroom trip I'd been warned about. The urge to jump. Just the evening before, while hanging out in a coffeehouse and smoking a bowl to calm my nerves after my international flight, I'd heard a story about a Japanese student-tourist on shrooms. He'd stripped naked and climbed out onto the railing of his 15th floor hotel balcony, held his arms out like wings, and jumped. He thought he could fly. Perhaps he'd met Vatsulu in bird form. Needless to say, the kid dropped like a rock and bounced down 15 flights of fire escape. Apparently he survived, but at the cost of multiple broken bones and splattered organs. I may have been drunk, stoned, and delirious, but I wasn't so far gone that jumping off a bridge to swim like a fish seemed like a good idea. I might go under and think I could breathe the water.

"Sorry Vatsulu, I'm going back to the hotel and going to bed," I declared over the railing.

"You don't have a choice," winked Vatsulu, and with that wink there was a flash of light.

I blinked out the blindness and shook my head. "Later tuna man," I insisted. Then I took a step back onto something slippery and squishy. I barely had time to look down and catch a glimpse of a banana peel under my shoe. Next thing I knew, I was tumbling over the rail, head over heels and into the water.

"HELP!"

Splash!

Chapter 3 – Sank like a rock

Help didn't come when I tumbled off the bridge and into the water. Vatsulu certainly wasn't any help. As I was drowning, he just swam around me in fast circles. As if it were all a joke, while I kicked and splashed for air, he did flips and turns and blew little bubbles of laughter. Each time I yelled "Help!" I choked down more water and sank deeper. I was suffocating, losing consciousness. I'd always been a good swimmer, but that afternoon I sure wasn't. Maybe it was the booze, or the hash, or the shrooms, or a combination thereof? After all, it had been hard enough to stagger about on my feet in such a state of intoxication, so maybe that explains why, despite my struggle to swim, I sank straight down and hit the bottom. I did the opposite of float.

This is the end of me, I thought. As it all began to fade, as my life began making an exit for death to take its place, I pondered. Well, at least I'd lasted as long as I had, I reminisced. I suppose it had been good life, I tried to convince myself. One last bubble escaped my nose and floated up, as if it were my very last thought. Then all went cold in my body and the blackness took my eyes...

It seemed forever before a shrieking sound in my ears startled me out of death, or my sleep, whichever state I was in.

"Wake up!"

"Eh?"

"Wake up! Johnny, wake up!" Insisted Vatsulu in a high-pitched voice.

I opened my eyes. Where was I? It looked like I was sitting right where I'd apparently drowned, at the bottom of the canal, but now the canal was empty. I could breathe! When I looked up, a ceiling of water appeared to be rushing overhead. Vatsulu was running circles around me. He was still orange with a human face, but now he had a dog's body.

"What the hell?"

"Johnny, you're a fish now. Your arms are fins and your legs are a tail. You're breathing water rather than air because your lungs have become gills."

I looked down over my body. I still had my hands and feet. No gills. It didn't make sense.

I shot Vatsulu an accusing glare.

Catching my beam, he stopped running and giggling and sat down in front of me. He perked his ears and tilted his head.

I replied with rolling eyes and a shrug.

"I know you still think of yourself as human, so that's the way you still see yourself – as human, but to me you look like a large salmon."

"To me, you look like a dog."

"Oh yeah, what kind of dog?" he smiled and perked his ears.

"A Boston Terrier."

Vatsulu's smile changed to a frown and his little pointed ears dropped. "Thanks a lot. I always thought of myself as being more of a Rottweiler."

"At least you're still man's best friend, but that doesn't help me much, now that I'm a fish and not a man. Does it?"

At my jest, Vatsulu's good cheer returned. He barked a few times in laughter, jumped up and ran a few circles around me, and then with perfect form did a back flip into my lap.

"Stop licking my face!" I screamed, as I fought to keep from getting the pink, sloppy tongue in my mouth. "Settle down boy!"

"Just trying to have some fun!" chuckle-growled Vatsulu, and then he flipped out of my lap to face me.

I wiped the spit and snot off my face and gave him another serious look. "What's *really* going on here?" I insisted.

Vatsulu tilted his head and lifted his ears as if shrugging, *don't ask me*.

Desperate to get a grip on the situation, I tried to answer for him: "Let me try to explain all of this based on what you've said and what's happened since I fell off the bridge: It looks like the water has turned into air and the air has turned into water, but it only appears that way because now I'm a fish. However, I still look like a man to my own eyes, only because I still think I'm a man. And you, though you are still a fish, you look like a dog."

"Well, not exactly," sighed Vatsulu. "I was trying to make this seemingly odd situation you've splashed into easier to understand. But, you aren't ever going to understand all of this in this life, so you have to accept things as they are, and flow with their apparent chaos and randomness. You can't ask, 'Where am I?' 'What is this?' 'Who are you?' 'Who are they?' 'How?' 'Why?' Or anything of the sort. There are no answers you will ever be able to comprehend in your current state. Instead of focusing on what you see and hear, smell and touch, the things you taste, listen to your gut. Accept what you perceive without skepticism or need for more. Seek questions without wanting to know their answers. Ask where to go next without seeking a place, a thing, or an explanation. Find your current and flow into it. You are a fish now. It is about swimming. It is about the flow. I know you still have more questions to ask. Just trust me when I tell you to quit asking for answers and to start seeking more questions without needing their answers. It is in the seeking of the question, not in the finding of the answer. The chasing of a firefly, not the catching of it."

"Nevertheless, let me try to answer a little bit better what you have been asking, just so you might be a little less leery of diving right into it all: Johnny, you are a man, a fish, and a dog, I am you, you are me, not to mention many other things. All that exists is now. There is no time. There is no future or past. Only now. And now you are all things and no thing, all at the same instant. Right now you are just fixated on being a man trapped in time. Like I told you, I have been a million things, but by saying *have been*, I was simply trying to communicate with you in terms of your faulty, time-centric perspective and language. The reality is that I am both a fish and a dog, right now, and so are you."

I scratched my head. "So we are both all things, right now?"

"That's right! And don't forget we are also no thing, right now."

I just sat there looking at him.

"At the cost of using faulty time-centric words, do you realize that you are never the same from one moment to the next?" the terrier enquired.

"Maybe," I shrugged, exhaled, inhaled, and tried to get my toes wet. "Is it kind of like how we are made of spinning atoms that are never positioned in the same way, or like how the cells in our bodies are either dying or dividing, so we are never exactly the same as before? But, even so, we still identify our ever-changing selves as our selves?"

Vatsulu nodded in approval and gave me a wink. Even I was impressed with my explanation. The shrooms were working! No wonder drugs were illegal where I was from – too much inspired abstract thinking could tear down the establishment. Sober masses need their priests and politicians to tell them of Heaven and Hell. Sober they lack the vision to see it for themselves; should they be intoxicated from within, they wouldn't need their clergy, politicians, or wives. There would be no nagging, taxes or tithes.

"Johnny," Vatsulu continued, "You seem so close to understanding the situation. This might be as close as you'll ever be to knowing the nature of your true, real substance, which is truly and really *no thing* at all. I want to emphasize the freedom and motion that is centric to this wondrous matter: Johnny, we are no thing, but we are also all things, or said another way, we are beings made of no thing and we swim through every thing, and it swims through us. It is only by being no thing that we are free to take any and all of the shapes and forms we may infinitely take among all the countless possibilities. On top of it all, all of this shape and form shifting is happening right now, all at the same time, so to say. Time is only a fiction that traps us into believing our changes must happen in any order, as if determined and numbered. *If this, then that, and if this, then that. If dog chases cat, then cat chases rat.*

There cannot be any freedom if *this* must lead to *that*, if the dog must chase the cat, but there is indeed freedom, Johnny. So *this* does not lead to *that*. The dog must not always be required to chase the cat. It must be able to choose not to chase the cat and to do something else. All possibilities must always be available to the dog, all at the same time, else the dog would not have a choice because it would have only one option: chasing the cat! No thing must never be lead to just a single thing; instead every thing must be possible to no thing, all at the same time. Otherwise freedom is not possible. One choice does not provide freedom, else we would chase the cat and that would be that!

To say it another way, there is no thing to lose, and every thing to gain. There is no thing to gain and every thing to lose. We are the same dog and we are not the same dog, all at the same time, and we do not have to chase the cat, though we may if it delights us, but we shall also sing and dance and take tea with our feline friend. For this to happen, all the possibilities of this feline-canine relationship must always be available. If time were real and the dog chased the cat, then the opportunity to take tea with the cat would be forever lost – trapped in history."

"Shit Vatsulu. My head is starting to hurt. I'm going to have to think about all this a while. Maybe a few more tangible examples would help? For instance, what would I see if I swam up and poked my head out into the air, er… water?" I pointed up.

"Most likely, everyone out there in the other world would look like a fish to you, but as I've been saying, everyone is every thing, right now, even though each of them is no thing. So, when you look at any one, they can appear to be any thing or every thing, or all things, but not no thing. It all depends on your perspective, and from your perspective, you are still a man, though you are in the water."

"But not no thing? I can't see others as no thing?"

"Exactly! Now tell me why you can't see you or me as no thing."

"Shit… well…" I did have a degree in Philosophy, so I ventured the obvious guess. "Because in being no thing we are simply empty vessels? Shells so to say. We can only manifest the substance or forms of the things we make a part of us?"

"Very good Johnny! That's the soul in a nutshell!"

"You mean empty shell?" I corrected. And just as a footnote to this hallucinogenic story, that was the first time I'd ever felt like I'd really grasped something about my very soul. It really was an empty thing that was tied to no thing – it was no thing. At most our souls were as a simple spec of dust, less than a mite. The soul is no thing and does nothing but allow us to point to me or to you, or any thing. Our fleeting consciousness is nothing at all: just a bunch of thoughts, memories, feelings, all tied to a spec of dust, a mite, a singular instance called our souls. We are nothing unless we are being, doing, living, dancing or singing about that little spec we know as ourselves, as me, as you. We are as little fleas with any thing and every thing mixing about us, becoming part of us, coming and going in so many varieties, endless possibilities. Or another way to look at it was that we are as ticks. Any thing and every thing are the things we suck up to fill our empty shells with blood, with fullness, until we swell so full we pop. We become little specs of dust again, nothing but no thing, and then we must find another host, more blood to suck up. This way we may become full again, again, at least until we pop, again.

Vatsulu was all smiles, if you've ever seen a Boston Terrier smile. By doing so he was sharing, or communing with my silent musings. I didn't have to ask if he was with my thoughts. I knew he was either reading them with me or was simply remembering once having had the same thoughts before, when they had danced about his spec of dust.

"Welcome to the other world, my friend," Vatsulu finally interrupted. "Adam was right about you."

I shook out of my stupor and looked up at him. "You mean welcome to every world and to any world?" I corrected. "And who is this Adam?"

Vatsulu's eyes brightened upon my words. "Johnny, you're quite the quick study, I must say. But be patient because there is much more to come, and we'll get to Adam, rather, we'll get you to Adam."

"Oh, alright…"

"Let's quit piddle-farting and get started. Time, as you say it, is wasting. We have a long journey ahead, so just follow me. We'll swim with the currents. That's how we'll find our way from one place to the next until getting to the end, though there really is no end."

"Where are we going?"

"No where in particular. We don't have to be any where, but we are every where now and we'll be every where eventually, even though we have already been there. Let's go!"

Vatsulu took off running along the bottom of the canal and I followed. After a few steps I lifted my feet and began swimming through the air, doing the breaststroke. Vatsulu turned back into a fish, and the air turned into water once more.

"Johnny?" Vatsulu yelled back at me in bubbles.

"Yeah?"

"I've got to go now. You'll never see me again, but I will always be every one you meet, even you!"

"What!"

"Just keep swimming my brother. Go with the currents."

And so Vatsulu vanished.

Chapter 4 – Bones to ashes and dust

I swam and swam. I closed my eyes as I swam with the flow. As I did so, the currents stripped me of my clothes and my shoes. As I swam I was also freed of all the other things I'd brought with me. The Baggage. My wake up to the alarm clock routine, dependence on a paycheck, the traffic, taxes, ex wives, parking tickets, debt collectors, bad television sitcoms, running out of toilet paper, of gas, having to piss or shit while stuck in traffic, angry girlfriends, looking older every time I saw myself in the bathroom mirror, every morning and every night when I flossed, brushed, and rinsed, and spat. All these things I should have abandoned long before I'd fallen off the bridge and into the water, a victim of Vatsulu's trickery. These were all things for the other world, the mundane; the things that didn't matter. By swimming with the currents, being purified, I was being given a second chance. It was all washed away, forgotten a stroke at a time, as if I had plunged into the water caked with filth and mire to be cleansed by the currents to which I trusted my body, and my soul. Cleansed of the other world, blessed with the deep onset of forgetfulness, I swam. I swam. Or maybe it wasn't swimming, but something else? Perhaps I was escaping? No, maybe I was becoming? Dying? Being born and living for the first time? So with closed eyes, I kept going, paddling and kicking, doing the breaststroke, remembering Vatsulu's words:

"Just keep swimming my brother. Go with the currents."

"Just keep swimming my brother. Go with the currents."

And so I went with the currents. I swam with the flow of the warm soothing water, and many rainbow colors flashed through my closed eyelids. I chased along cooler flows which were filled with music and sound, and most of it I didn't recognize, though it ranged from tweeting birds to banging African drums, to Brahms, and Chopin. I swam.

I opened my eyes 10,000 strokes later, and discovered I was no longer in a canal, but deep in the middle of an ocean with no land in sight, nor was there any bottom, but I wasn't alone. There were fish, whales, dolphins, and sharks. The dolphins were spinning circles around the whales, and the sharks were chasing and swallowing the fish, chewing them up, shitting them out whole again, but in new shapes and sizes and colors. If a victim went in a stout silver fish, it might come back out the other end a long red one, or as a baby octopus, or as a dolphin.

And then from nowhere, with no warning, a giant mouth opened up and swallowed me whole! In one big gulp, I was quickly startled from my amazement and tranquility and captured by fear.

"Oh shit. Johnny and the whale…"

All I could do was roll into a ball and brace myself for the crunching teeth, but they never came. I was spared by a hard second gulp, and down the giant throat I twisted and rolled until with a tight contraction and release I was spat into a dark chamber. Out of the gullet and into the stomach? To my surprise, my next encounter was not with bile. The water rushed out and a multi-hued light came on. I blinked a few times, shook the water from my face, and cleared my eyes, finding myself sitting on the floor of a little round cavern with fleshy walls, ceiling and floor. The multi-hued light emanated from a little stained glass dragonfly lamp, and Renaissance style paintings adorned the fleshy walls. Most were scenes involving satyrs and nymphs, jugglers or dwarves, brides, dryads, ogres, and yellow-eyed wolves lurking in the shadows. A small bed was in the room. A large shell served as its canopy and sparkling coral its frame. I blinked again and my eyes nearly popped from their sockets! A beautiful girl with long red hair was sitting in a Windsor rocking chair at a little ornate desk. She was buxom and naked from head to toe, sitting on one foot and slowly rocking herself with the other. A pencil and a small book were in her hands. She stopped reading, brushed her dangling hair aside, and looked up over the top of her little round glasses at me.

"What are you doing in my house?" she asked plainly.

"I was swallowed by a whale."

"I see," she said, and then she put down her things, hopped out of her chair and onto her back on the bed. She opened her legs wide, so I could see the white soles of her dainty feet, and then she lifted her head and looked down at me over her ripe breasts, smooth porcelain belly, and great big mound of curly pubic hair. It matched the hair on her head. "It must be that time of year for me," she said.

My silence, bulging eyes, and dropped jaw were my only answer. I was overwhelmed and confused.

"We have been brought together to mate," she plainly declared, but after I kept standing there with nothing to say, she gave me a crooked smile and a wink, and opened her legs wider.

It was too much to bear, and soon my anxiety was overtaken by desire. Her raising her hips off the bed and gyrating for me was an obvious mating call. But something inside me made me resist stepping forward and ravaging her, which was a first for me. There she was, a poised and ready young tart, with sweet nectar dripping from her pinkness. It was enough to make even an old man feel desire for flesh again, but my feet were just too heavy. It was a miracle of self restraint, as if someone had taken control of my body, like another me possessing previously unknown wisdom and strength. Maybe I'd finally found my conscience?

"Come on!" she gestured. "Just put that thing in here," she pointed. "It won't hurt, not at first. When you feel the sting, you'll already be finished."

"I can't."

"It sure looks like you can! All you have to do is take a few steps forward and climb on top! I'll put it in for you and do the rest. I'll suck it all right out of you and into my tummy! I know I said it would hurt a little, but it will feel really nice just the same."

"I can't."

"Are you sure?"

"Yes."

"Good!" she squealed and clapped, slapped her legs back together and hopped to her feet. With a dainty hand held out she approached me. I accepted her offer and shook. It was a formal handshake, as if we'd just made a deal and sealed it.

"You passed the test!" she proclaimed.

"What test?"

"You are a man with more to pass on than bones to ashes and dust."

Another riddle. Shit. I began to regret not taking the bait. I wanted to ask questions, but what was the use? Alright Vatsulu. Go with the flow.

"Let's go!" She squealed and clapped.

The water started rushing in. Her legs melted into a fish tail and she took me by the hands. "You won't be able to breathe under water any more, so you need to take a deep breath and hold on to me. Just keep your arms around me – don't let go, and I'll do the same. Put your mouth on my nipple and keep it there," she pointed. "You'll have to breathe through me," she giggled. "I might jump a little at first because it will tickle, but just keep breathing!" And so we were enveloped by the ocean, fell into one-another's arms, and I began taking my breath from her. As I clung to her, she took me off my feet by moving her hips. We swam. She swam. We swam out of the behemoth's mouth, and into the depths of the sea. I couldn't see where we were going because her breasts were in the way, but I could tell we were swimming downward.

"I have a friend you need to meet," she gurgled into my ear. "It will be a long swim because the bottom is a long way down. You can go to sleep if you want. I won't let go of you."

And as she swam I fell asleep, and it was a pleasant slumber. I dreamt she reached down and stroked me with the softest touch, until I was spilling a milky trail, and into its flow she dropped many eggs. They were little translucent eggs which popped right out of her, as slowly gyrated her hips and wagged her tail. One by one the eggs burst into fireflies.

In her embrace, I dreamt the many stories I would one day tell. They appeared to me as if I were center stage of each of them, among the characters and props, hearing every word and narration, the detail of every scene down to the specs of dust floating in light beams surrounded by darkness. It was amazing how much was born from that slumber, as I took air from her, slept in her embrace, dreamt many dreams, had visions, moved with her as if I were a part of her, as her delicate rhythm became one with me, as my flesh became hers and hers became mine.

When I awoke, she was gone. I was sitting before a stone sarcophagus in an ancient stone room, and there was only one way in or out: a tall portal between two pillars, and spiraling stairs leading up to it.

In the sarcophagus, in the middle of the floor, a decaying skeleton was lying on its side.

Nothing but bones and dust.

Chapter 5 – All that remains of me

And there I was, sitting in a crypt on a stone floor, staring into an ancient sarcophagus, gazing upon the remains of a crumbling skeleton. I was beneath an ocean somewhere far away. Perhaps it was another dimension, a state of death, or my mind trying to find its way out of a coma? I had no clothes. I was completely naked in so many ways. I had no way to reach out to anyone because they were unreachable, beyond the veil, in another world, the other world now. The few friends I'd made along the way had abandoned me. Vatsulu and the red-haired mermaid were gone. I was alone, far from home. Home? Would I ever find my way back to it? Wine? Would I ever have another drink? Women, would I ever take another one to bed? Everything, even my memories, suddenly seemed so distant, or unreal, as did my hopes for the future. Perhaps I'd traveled so far into something else I was no longer myself? Maybe I was nothing? No, maybe I was no thing? What had Vatsulu said about that?

I pondered.

Think about it. We aren't ever the same person from one day to the next, or from one second to the other. We are always some thing else or no thing on its way to being or becoming yet another some thing else, in constant flux. Sometimes we try too hard to just be one thing and to name it our self, but we are not stagnant things. We are beings, not stones. We are being a million other changing things at this very instant. Or maybe a trillion? To resist this flux is like trying to stop our hearts from beating, our lungs from breathing, and as a result we will suffer and die.

I'd always been in flux, but until I fell off the bridge I had assumed it was a character disorder. I had always been a walking contradiction. Once I'd been a churchgoing fellow, and had really believed. Now I wasn't religious and questioned the gods. I'd once fallen in love with a girl and married her. We were "soul mates," we used to swear. Now she was in another man's arms. I'd lived in the snow, the desert, the mountains, and near an ocean, and had lived a different life in each place. I'd had a lot of friends, but had lost most of them along the way, only to gain new ones wherever I turned up next. Some old friends had known me as a prankster while others knew me as a rather severe fellow. Some girls had known me as a hot lover, while others believed I was a stick in the mud. Wasn't it peculiar how I was always a different person in every place I'd been? In one place I'd made my living as a bouncer. I was a rough, tough guy. In another, I'd been a lawyer. I was a briefcase, a talking suit and tie. I'd been a student, a boyfriend, a husband, a lover, a hater, a good employee, a bad employee, a loyal friend, a scoundrel, a thief, a savior, a good son, a bad son, an aspiring, alcoholic writer falling apart at the seams, a guy with it all together and sturdy as a granite pillar, and then again a guy with nothing but everything crumbling down around him.

Hell, what was I? All of it? None of it? All of it at once? Time, distance, sentiment, belief, hope, happiness, and sorrow, loss and gain – all of it can seemingly change us into something entirely different than before, down to the quick, from one day to the next, one second to the next. Who I am? It is always something else other than what I'd been a million times before. Or have I been it before? Or what I shall be once more? We are no thing and no thing is every thing, or it can be, or will be, even if we try to resist it. Is that what Vastulu said?

I realized.

I am all of what I have been, what I am currently being, and what I will ever be or could be, all at the same time. Somehow, it was all tied together, into me – attached by something, be it spirit, memory, tendons, spider webs, or the branches of trees, the stars in the sky. My gut just told me so, whispered it to me, and I knew it, however fleeting, intangible, or ineffable it was. Vatsulu was starting to make sense. No thing is every thing, and every thing isn't no thing. But it can be. It depends on who is looking in the mirror and who is looking back, and whether we are in the other world, in a dream, in Heaven, Hell, or the mundane. When I look into a mirror, my face never looks exactly as I remembered it; yet, I still recognize it as my face. It always reflects back the same expression I offer. Should I make a smiling face, I am returned a smiling face. Should I give a sad face, a sad face is reflected. A smile in the mirror makes me smile back again. A frown a frown. There is no more to it than that.

No more questions, please. Now I've realized I've told you all the secrets a number of times already, and this story has barely started. Quit seeking answers and find the bigger questions. Chase after the fireflies but do not catch them. Admire their blinking beauty, and move on. Don't get tangled in any riddle, smoke, or fog. Don't ever grab hold of any thing and refuse to let go of it. Keep becoming what you are becoming next, be what you are being, else you may trip and fall.

I stood up and explored the crypt, a one room chamber with a vaulted ceiling and a polished stone floor. Spiraling stairs lead up to an exit between two pillars, the only way out. Flaming torches adorned the walls and their flickering flames made shadows dance about the vault. In the middle of it all was a crumbling skeleton, lying on his side in an open sarcophagus.

I bent down and examined the skeleton. It was in a fetal position, as if trying to guard its remaining bones from harm. The bones were brittle and porous, and had turned dark brown. The finger and toe bones had all but disintegrated, as had a few ribs and vertebrae, but the skull and its teeth were still intact. Slowly, I reached into the sarcophagus, and just as my fingertip touched a bony knuckle, the knuckle crumbled to dust.

"Ouch!" yelled the skull's mandible.

"Shit!" I jumped back. "Shit!"

The jaw kept moving. My heart raced, my eyes bulged, and my jaw dropped.

"That's right! I'm a talking skeleton! And you can't believe it!" dust swirled around him as he spoke. "I can't believe it either. So, get over it.

Get closer and listen up. I used to be a man like you, and I still am in small part. I've still got bones, even though they are crumbling. I'm just missing the flesh and blood. That's all."

I just stood there, still speechless, heart racing, eyes bulging, mouth hanging open.

"Flesh got your tongue?" chuckled the skeleton with its flapping lower jaw. "I understand. Anyway, I already know your name. It's Johnny. Don't ask how I know. I just do. You can call me Adam because I'm the oldest remains of any man that's ever lived. And no, I'm not *The Adam* of the Bible either. I doubt anyone was or is. But who knows or cares about that? I just think I've earned the right to be called Adam because, as I said, I'm the oldest remains of any man there ever was. And for this same reason, I'm going to be your guide. Well, I won't actually guide you because I can't stand and walk. All I can do is talk you through the steps you'll be taking on your journey. Well, actually, you won't see me again, or hear from me, until you get back, that is, if you get back. Now listen! My words are limited. Just talking will kill me a little faster than I'm already dying – decaying actually, because I'm already dead. You've seen how easily I break into dust. Just flapping my jaw makes me crumble away faster. So, remember all my words and don't waste them. Ask me to repeat something and it might take away something else I could have told you."

I finally mustered the courage to speak. "Wh…w…why…why h… have you remained… er… um, alive – I mean around – for so long?"

"Now that is the question, isn't it? I must have really been something when I had flesh on my weary bones, huh?" flapped his mandible which swirled the dust some more. "In fact, I am here now exactly because I was nothing, rather than something, when I had flesh on my bones. Actually I was only one thing… Anyway, what you see is all that remains of me because when the end of my fleshy days came, when I died, as you call it, all I had to leave behind was my body. It was all I had to offer. The flesh rotted away, and here I am, nothing but bones. Still taking up space. This is it. That is it. These damn bones are all I ever had to say or do, or be. I became nothing else. I'm a carcass. I left nothing behind but a carcass. Even when I was as you are now, I was no thing but an animated carcass. Granted, I had more flesh than I do now, but I was still a carcass. So, I'm being eternally punished for being so greedy – keeping me all to myself and never doing anything with it."

"Who is punishing you?"

"Me! Can't you see? I'm the punisher and the punished."

"Then why are you my guide?"

"Actually, I'm not your guide. I'm just sending you on a mission. That's all. Figure the rest out your own self. And to answer your question, I'm your *guide* because I know better than anyone how to avoid my mistake. I've contemplated it longer than anyone else could have, for I am the oldest remains of any living man, well, dead one anyway, but you know what I mean. Obviously, I'm the most experienced and learned in the subject. So, you are my disciple now. You will also be my atonement. In the end, if you survive this mission and make it back to me, you will bring me flowers. I will smell them in one last big whiff, and then you will crush my bones into ashes and dust."

Chapter 6 – Scorpion on my back

"Why would I want to crush your bones into ashes and dust!" I blurted. It seemed to me Adam should be sending me on a quest to get his flesh back, not turn what little was left of him into powder, ashes and dust.

"Johnny, I thought you'd learned to seek questions, not answers? Don't disappoint me after you've come so far."

"Adam, I feel like I've heard this before. How do you know all of this? You've been talking to Vatsulu! Haven't you?" Just as I was asking, I already knew it was a stupid question. I was talking to a guy who had been around a long, long time...

"When you've been around as long as me, you know things, even before they are spoken. Don't make me say it again. Seek questions. Not answers. Find a question and let it lead to the next question before you hear an answer. Go with the flow is the old cliché. Swim with the currents, as our good old friend Vatsulu prescribes."

Of course he had been talking to Vatsulu! Vatsulu had mentioned Adam before, and had started me on the path towards meeting Adam. But which of them was the teacher, and which of them the student, I wondered? I wasn't going to ask. It didn't matter because both of them were teaching the same principles:

Embrace the asking of "Why?" But do not seek the end of your question, which is its answer. Just plead for it. Just go with it. Just flow with it. Swim with the currents, as Vatsulu had taught me, as Adam was now re-emphasizing, as the red-haired mermaid had shown me. Sometimes you just have to let go, stop seeking answers, or worrying about what's ahead. Just close your eyes and breathe through her nipple, and she will carry you deeper into the mystery. Questions should lead to more questions and never any answers. Answers are false ends to questions. They will paralyze you with fear, satiate you, give you the illusion your work is finished, that there is no need to swim any farther. We can never stop swimming, else we would not exist, because, after all, we are no thing. Only by continually swimming through every thing do we exist as some thing from one thing to the next, to the next, as it all, every thing, is in flux and flowing through us as we flow through it, flinging and flashing and flailing in chaotic frenzy. We sing and we dance.

"I don't have anything else to ask," I resolved, sat down before Adam, and waited for his question.

"Are you ready?"

"Yes."

"Embrace every burden," his bony, lower jaw flapped. "Every step is precious because you only have so many to take," arose the dust with his words. "Of every 10,000 steps you take, only 1 one of them will put your foot on some thing, and you'll only be able to stand there for a moment, before having to continue along. In that 10,000th place, you might leave a footprint, but the wind and rain will quickly wash and blow away the proof you were once there. When you take that 10,000th step, leave more than a footprint. Cut off and abandon a part of your body there. Make it a granite pillar impervious to wind and rain, unlike a mere foot's impression left to dissipate in sand. But remember: leave just a part of your body there, not your entire being."

His very words cast a spell. Light filled the sub-oceanic vault, as did intense heat. I shaded my eyes, stood, and turned around. A portal had appeared behind me, and through it I could see a vast desert – nothing but sand dunes and scorching sun all the way to the horizon.

"Get going before it closes up!" insisted Adam.

I clinched my teeth, bore down on the fear in my gut, and took a daring leap. I just made the plunge without thinking.

I landed ankle deep in the sand, and the portal disappeared behind me. My soles began to burn with an intensity I can't describe, as did the skin all over my body. The sensation was beyond the realm of pain, and it was as if I'd done nothing less than dive straight into a 10,000 degree oven! Instantly my mouth dried, my tongue shriveled up, and my eyes collapsed. I was only able to inhale one scorching breath before my throat burned shut and my lungs turned to ash. It was as if the desert had stabbed a straw into me and violently sucked out every drop of blood, sweat and piss, and then spat fire back through my every sinew, vein, and pore. I'd been in desert heat before, but this was more than a desert. So this is Hell? I couldn't breathe and began to suffocate. I became dizzy and began stumbling around. Sand-filled wind lashed my body about. Blinded and choked, I was helpless, all my strength sapped. I lost balance when I stepped out of the cooked meat that had once been my feet, collapsed, and fell face first into a dune. As I lay there losing consciousness, I felt the flesh on my back burning off, drying up, cracking, peeling away, joining the wind and grit, exposing my spine and my ribs so my boiling organs could start broiling. It didn't hurt so badly because my nerves were so cooked, but that didn't make my predicament any easier to bear. So was this Hell? It didn't matter. What could I do? It was either a test or it was my end, devised by a sinister trickster.

I thought for sure it was the end when I felt something stab deeply into my neck. But then I felt something cool and soothing rushing into what remained of my mummified body. Quickly the heat and the elements became less intense, and the wind quit stripping the remnants of my flesh from the bones. It seemed I was being re-inflated with life after nearly becoming a skeleton like Adam. Whatever was being pumped into me through my neck flowed through and filled all my sinews and bones, restored not only my lifeblood, but also my muscles and skin. Suddenly, my strength and total consciousness returned, allowing me to climb to my feet with ease, even open my new eyes. I could see again, but even clearer! I realized I had been changed. Did I feel stronger? Smarter? Every sense and every thought seemed enhanced. The intense sunlight no longer blinded me, and the wind and the heat were now bearable. However, one thing was of major concern. Something heavy was clinging to my shoulder; that something which had stabbed into my neck and returned me to life was still there, on me. I turned my head and found myself face-to-face with a black scorpion the size of a large cat. Its 8 polished eyes glinted, as did its carapace, and its sharp feet were burrowed into my shoulder, neck, and arm. The tail disappeared behind me and I surmised that its sharp tip, the stinger, had been plunged into my neck and was still there.

Somehow, I felt no fear. I knew I had to walk. I had to carry the scorpion with me. It had returned the flesh to my bones, so I would accept it as a friend without asking why. Don't ask why. Go with the currents. Start taking steps. Count your steps. That was it! So I began counting. 10,000 steps it had been said. 10,000 steps.

1, 2, 3…

50…

200…

Here and there, my skepticism stopped me and I just stood there. Whenever I did so, I'd turn and look at the scorpion and it became heavier. The glinting, 8 black eyes began to frighten me, and my flesh once again began burning in the wind, sun, and sand. My legs became weaker. Only by continuing to walk, counting my steps, did I lose the fear again. Only by walking did the scorpion's nectar flow freely through my veins, heal me, and protect my body from the elements. I had no time to stop and ponder, to ask questions for answers' sake.

I kept counting, 330, 331, 332…

And counting, 2000, 3000, 4000…

As I continued counting, I pondered the absurd rhythm of walking. I was going somewhere, and didn't know where. It didn't matter. I was moving, going, being. There was something to the simple rhythm of walking, traversing the desert, the action of it, my bearing the scorpion, carrying its weight in return for its life-giving poison. There was meaning in it all, but I could only feel it in my gut, not describe it; I had to have faith in it, and to question it not. To ask of it, "Why?" was to find its visceral essence and strength dissipating. To ask "Why" is to stop seeking because you are insisting on an immediate answer instead of taking another step towards it. The meaning of it all had to be sought, not captured. Only chased. Like a blinking firefly in the blackness. To ask "Why?" was to try and capture it, not to follow after it, to be lead. It was only through my savage intuition, that feeling in my gut and not in my head, that I could continue on. All other devices of mind and logic would allow its escape, insist I stop in my tracks to try and solve riddles. Jar the firefly. Logic and mind, I knew in my muscle and bone, and not in my brain, would abandon me to death in the desert. Keep going, keep counting. Don't jar the firefly.

9998, 9999, 10,000…

I was tempted to stop at 10,000, but I didn't ask why nothing happened when I got there. I just kept walking, bearing that scorpion on my back. Counting.

10,001, 10,002, 10,003…

And it wasn't how many steps I took that mattered, I realized. So I kept walking, and after a while I stopped counting. The sun sat and rose, and the sun sat and rose again. And I continued walking. Perhaps the days and nights came 10,000 times, but it didn't matter. Maybe it was at 10,000 years something was supposed to happen? And as I continued and continued, the scorpion became a part of me, much like an arm or a leg. The trance and rhythm of the walking was all I needed, and with it I was complete, moving, being. Infinite time could pass without worry. I found peace, not intellectually or in my heart, but in my gut. It just washed over me and through me and I cannot tell you why or how it happened. All I can tell you is that once peace came to me and became part of me, I finally took my 10,000th step. Only when I found peace and allowed it to infuse my being did the ziggurat appear on the horizon. It was a great monument made of stone pillars and stairs reaching upward into the heavens. At the top of the mighty temple stood a 1000'+ tall bronze deity, adorned in gold. It had a scorpion's tail and several arms, 2 across its breasts, the other 6 akimbo. Her almost androgynous and smooth 8-eyed face offered kindness. Only her chin moved as I approached. It was moving slowly downward, allowing her 8 large glinting eyes to follow me, to focus her silver pupils on my face as I climbed the sandstone stairs towards her.

I prostrated myself at the great goddess's feet.

I did not pray, but listened. I knew not to ask a question, but to wait for the next question to come to my patient ears, so that I would receive guidance and direction, my next destination to yet another place, time, or being.

The sun sat, the night passed, and the sun rose at dawn.

From above a feminine voice finally whispered, "Become a pillar."

I stood, bowed before the great bronze god, and looked up at her. She slowly opened her embracing arms and hands and revealed her breasts. She smiled upon me and I was overtaken by some invisible force, as if a mist of living clouds had embraced me and poured into me through my mouth, nose, and every pore. I suddenly felt completely protected, safe, and no longer lost. I smiled up at her, bowed, turned away, and descended the stairs of her platform.

I searched the ziggurat until finding a missing column. I stepped into that 10,000th place, folded my arms, looked out across the desert, and smiled.

My flesh grew tall and turned to stone.

I became a pillar.

Chapter 7 – Off the pedestal

I stood there a pillar.

And I came to know time through the being and essence of stone. Stone, more than most any other thing, has been every thing before, but seldom is stone no thing, and it is even rarer for no thing to be stone. The true self can almost be grasped when it becomes stone, but not quite. Being stone may give us insight into being a particular thing, though it hinders our becoming other things or being them. In the other world many things are made of stone-like substance, or appear to be made of it, but it is not real stone in the other world. It is only bone.

I stood there a pillar.

And slowly did I become just stone and no thing else. So much so that with every blink of my eyes, the seasons changed – while all else raced around me, my heartbeat was counted in years rather than seconds, allowing me first insights into nature's chaotic serendipity of changing colors and contours. The desert about me vanished. Winter flashed into being in all of its blanketed whiteness. Just close my eyes and open them again to find the falling snow had melted, instantly transformed into sunshine and blue skies, green grassy fields. Wink again and I was amidst a hailstorm, flashing lighting and screaming thunder, and again in a snap, in a blink, there was darkness all around, but for the vast constellations glimmering above, which occasionally made a show of their changing moons, fiery comets and falling stars. Fall asleep and arise once more to find the desert returned, or look away and back again, and again it was changed into grassy, rolling hills; wide rivers slowly flowing with fish springing out into the air and splashing back into the blue waters again. Look down at your feet and back up again, and discover you are suddenly surrounded by pine trees, deciduous forest, jungle or marsh, or foothills rolling up into mountains. Each time the wind and rain withered it all away for something new, making way for the earth to give birth to yet other changing landscapes. So much passed before me, perhaps tens of thousands of years, or a million, but then one day, or should I say one time? No. Not one day or one time, but something else. Nevertheless, the desert returned a final time, and I was still standing there – a pillar – and my heartbeat once again quickened. And so every thing had made several rounds, had been all things, and I had stood there watching the chaotic dance of it all, the serendipity, all the shapes and transformations, mutations, combinations, permutations, coagulations, transmutations, come together, mix, go apart and blend collectively, return, disappear, reappear, and manifest a million faces with a million infinite expressions. During this time, I had been no thing but stone, not bone. A pillar.

I still stood there a pillar.

Waiting.

I searched the horizon, where the sand and sky drew a line of blue ether against sandy earth. After many years, I spotted something in the distance. It was a black snake wiggling through the sand my way. At the end of its laborious journey, it slithered up the steps and to the base of me, or should I say what used to be my feet? It raised its head on its long neck, showed its fangs, and spoke,

"Hello Johnny."

"Don't tell me I'm not supposed to ask how you know my name. Besides, how can you recognize me because I'm no longer a man, but a pillar?"

"You aren't much of a man after being a pillar for so many epochs, it is true, but I sssssuppose it is a ssssstate of mind. Bessssides, I don't recognize formsssss. I recognize esssssencesssss, which are the no thingsssss of each of usssss, ssssstone or flesssssh, or bone, or not. "

"I thought it was a state of being? No thing? And you say essence?"

"Wordsssss, words, wordsssss…" hissed the snake. "Nevertheless, your naïveté makesssss it clear you still don't undersssssstand, even though you've witnesssssssed the passsssssing of an entire round, or a countlesssss number of them. You are ssssstill sssso far from grassssssping it, far from it sssstill. But it makesssss sssssense. You've just been sssstanding there like an imbecile for immeassssurable time, not doing a thing from one round to the next."

"Grasping what? Imbecile!"

"The going roundsssss of roundsssss. You big dummy!"

"Round? Dummy!" Now this snake was really insulting me. If I'd only had arms or legs, I'd have strangled or stomped the fucking viper. But I only had ears.

"Yesssss, round. During your sssstay here, all things have been and become every permutation of all posssssibilities, and now they are sssstarting over again. In fact, sssince you've been here, sssseveral infinite rounds have been made by mossssst thingsssss, and at leasssst a couple countlesssss roundsssss have been made by all the others, that isssss, with one exception. I think that may be the problem."

"Don't tell me. I get what you are saying. I've remained a pillar and haven't changed at all, while everything else was making the rounds."

"Making the round to be precissssse, so forgive my having missssspoken," the snake corrected. "There really isssss only one of them that keepsssss repeating."

"Whatever."

"Just a minor correction for both of usssss. Otherwise I'm quite impresssssed by what you've learned. Vatsulu said you were sssssharp. I couldn't have said it better myself, had I been no thing but a pillar, a sssstone thing, for sssso long."

"Vatsulu? You know him?"

"Yesssss, hissed the snake. Vatssssssulu. I had a chat with him before I ate him."

"Ate him!"

"Don't worry. I know he was dear to you, but he went in and came out again, became sssssomething else, jusssssst as we all have before, and who knows when he will become a devouring sssssnake and I will be the moussssse he is eating? After all, there is no escaping it. I suppose you can call it fate, or just the inevitable inesssscapability of the randomness and chaos that tearsssss it all apart and putsssss it all together again, just as it always has been. We all get to make the round, in all the waysssss the round comesssss, over and over."

"If that's the case, and there's no beginning or end to any of this, Vatsulu has eaten us both many times before, and he'll do it again!"

"Vatsssssulu said you were sharp! I must ssssssay it again! That'sssssssss right, and we have already eaten him before and will be eating him again."

"But wait! If we live right, can't we escape this cycle?"

"No, who told you that?"

"Religions that believe in reincarnation often say you can break out of the cycle."

"Sssssooooo ssssssilly. Don't lissssssten to everything you hear, even though you've heard it before and will hear it again," chuckled the snake.

"I don't know if I buy all this."

"Don't look at me. I'm just a sssssssssnake, at leassssssssst for the time being."

"Pardon my skepticism, but why don't I remember any of this stuff ever happening before?"

"You will remember it, eventually, and you have remembered it before. You're just ssssssstuck on memories of being a pillar, or a Johnny. In fact, even asssss a pillar you are sssstill thinking of yoursssssself asssss 'Johnny.'"

"Wait a minute here. If it is all in flux, then how come my name isn't in flux? That's remained the same. I keep being called 'Johnny'"

"That'sssss part of the problem, and that'sssss why I'm paying you a visssssit. As I sssssaid, you are the only one left who hasssssn't gone an entire round, at leasssssst thissssss time around. The problem issss partially connected to your inssssssisting that you are Johnny and can't be anything or anyone elsssse. Anyway, sssssstop asssssssking questionssssss!"

I'd always liked Philosophy, and what the snake was saying made sense in a logical loop sort of way. But what if it was a trick? Snakes. They were always tricksters in all the stories I'd read. Yes. That was it! This was a trick! I was being tested by Adam, or maybe by Vatsulu? Maybe the snake was one of them!

"I'm not buying it. I'm staying put."

"Ok... ok..." hissed the snake. "Have it your way. Just don't come crying to me when you sssssuffer the consequencesssss. I don't want to have to tell you, 'I told you sssssso.'"

"Go bug another pillar."

"I can't. You are the only one left. Asssss I sssssaid, all the othersssss have had their turnsssss asssss pillarsssss and are waiting for you to join them in becoming sssssomething elssssse."

"Sorry lizard. I'm staying put."

The snake hissed, turned around, and slithered away.

Night fell and morning came again, as did the snake, slithering up to my feet, raising its head, and showing its fangs.

"Hey Johnny," hissed the snake, "I hear you were once a ladiessss' man. Back when you were a man."

The beast did seem a bit lonely, from the look in its cold, black eyes, and I felt a little lonely too. At least the reptile was now on another subject, and I hadn't had a normal conversation in perhaps a million years. Besides, I was a pillar and it was a snake. I was safe, all wrapped up in stone. The company was welcome. A little chat would be harmless, if I remained a pillar.

"No. Not really. They came and went."

"Yeah? What kindsssss of girlsssss did you like?"

"I liked all kinds, as long as they weren't too fat or diseased. The crazy ones always had a special allure."

"What about your dream girl?"

"Hell, I don't know. They all caused a lot of trouble. I'm not sure I have one anymore."

"Ok. Indulge me. Tell me what the ideal girl looksssss like. Use your imagination! Give me a fantassssssy! Whatever you fancy right now. What would sssssshe be like?"

"It all depends on my mood, so right now, it would be one with long red hair, smiles a lot…" I began to ponder, hmm. I hadn't conjured up such a fantasy girl in a while. "Put her in a short sundress…" Yeah, that's it. Now it was getting better. And with women there had to be wine. "A bottle of chardonnay is in one of her hands and…" I closed my eyes to focus on the details. "…and, I got it!" I blurted, just as I popped my eyes back open.

The snake was gone, but the girl I'd just described was standing there, in the flesh, in a short sundress and with a lot of long leg. A bottle of chardonnay was in one of her hands, and the hem of her dress was in the other.

"Hey cutie pie," she smiled, as she lifted the hem to reveal missing panties. "I bet you're thirsty!"

Yeah, you know what happens next. I fell for the old snake in the garden trick. Funny how in life we have these great epiphanies and feel we are transforming into something else, or have already done so – turned into something truly meaningful or profound. Then along comes a girl in a short summer dress, lifts it up and offers some wine. You can see the shallow trick from miles away, but somehow it's always so easy to give it all up and take the bait. Such an easy trick even a dumb snake can pull it off, and which snake is it, really? Eternity is so easily and ignorantly given away for a temporary drunken countenance, or for the murderous explosion that comes from having a pretty girl's soft heels pressing into our clinching buttocks until we can't take it any longer. When we sober up, we are empty of drink and everything else, having poured it all away into our bladders to piss it out, or having spewed it all into the depths of her belly – and now all but the headache is gone. It is so easy to live and die. It is so easy to be as Adam and lose all our flesh, to end up no thing once again.

My stone body lost its height and turned to flesh. With bare feet I stepped down from my indelible pedestal and into hot sand to make temporary footprints.

Chapter 8 – Journey to Hades

I left footprints in the sand, and the wind blew them away, as I drank Chardonnay, and sang songs, and danced with a girl in a sundress. I have to admit it was a good time, at least for the time being. Sometimes throwing it all away seems worth it. There can be joy in being as a comet, speeding through the universe at the cost of burning your body away, until there is no more left to cast off into a bright, blazing tail. Until we are no thing again? If you don't spend your flesh getting somewhere, you'll never go anywhere. You'll be as a fat Buddha sitting in the same place until the end of time, doing nothing but embracing your swollen belly and staring into nothingness. You'll be as a pillar, not as a comet.

As I lay there on top of the girl in the sand, my belly large with wine, my back streaked with sweat, and my loins spent, she turned back into the snake.

"Ouch, ouch!" hissed the snake. "Get off of me you big oaf! You're too heavy!"

I rolled off and into the sand and felt sick to my stomach. Had I just committed an act of bestiality? Luckily I was drunk and half conscious, or the sudden realization of how heinous a crime I'd just committed would have been much worse. Wine is a gift from the gods.

"You tricked me!" I whimpered.

"Oh, sssshut up you idiot," you knew what you were doing.

"I screwed a snake!"

"Do I have to call you an idiot again? Look, you really did drink and make merry with a girl, a real flesssssh and blood human girl. I wasssss asssss much a girl in the flesssssh asssss any real girl can ever be. In fact, I was of real girl flesssssh, and was wearing real girl perfume."

"But you are a snake!"

"Sssso what? You've been a snake with a lot of women. Payback isssss a bitch, eh? Ssssso don't cassssst the first sssstone. Of courssssse you weren't a sssssnake in body when you were with them – you were a man in the flesssssh, but you were a sssssnake in sssssspirit. I wasssss likewissssse – a girl in the flesssssh, but just plain old me, a sssssnake, in sssssspirit."

"Payback… …I suppose what goes around really comes around."

"Yep. Eventually. And Johnny, if it isssss of any consssssolation, I am a girl sssssnake."

"Really?" I sighed with relief. My stomach started to feel a little better, and my curiosity returned. I couldn't resist asking the obvious next question,

"Snake?"

"Yeah Johnny?"

"Was it any good?"

"What? The sssssex?"

"Yeah, the sex."

"Bad sssssex isssss sssstill good sssssex, but you were a little rough. I could have ussssed sssssome foreplay."

"I'll keep that in mind next time."

With that, the snake slithered away. She just left me there, lying in the sand next to the ziggurat I'd abandoned. In the corner of my eye, the bonze goddess in gold adornment glinted, as the brightening sunlight became hotter and hotter and hotter. I did not dare turn my face directly to her. I knew she had once again covered her breasts and her smile was gone, her face returned to its former stoicism. I feared she was disappointed in me for abandoning her eternity just for a temporary frolic with a snake. Perhaps she was causing the desert to suddenly become so hot again, just like it had been when I'd first stepped into it. Like before, my flesh began to sizzle and bubble. It peeled off as the wind swept it away to reveal my bones. All I could do was kick and scream as my flesh was cooked and stripped, as I became like Adam. When the job was finished, my bleached bones lay in the sand, my lower jaw flapping, "Oh god, this is worse than a hangover. Woe is me! Shit…"

When you are a skeleton, you have no flesh. And it is flesh that gives you a sense of time. When we are of flesh, the stomach becomes hungry for breakfast at morning, the eyes sleepy at night. Bones, they just lay there, never desiring sustenance and only aware of now, not the past, and not the future. The skull's sockets are oblivious to light or darkness when the eyes are missing. I don't know how much time passed before the scorpion returned, gathered up my bones, and carried me back to Adam. But during this time I probably reviewed my life a million times, maybe a billion, and the odd thing I discovered is that no matter how many times I mulled over and pondered it all, it all remained shrouded in mystery. I am fairly certain that man's primal questions will never be answered. Where did the gods come from, if there are any gods? How many gods are there? What is my purpose? Why are there stars in the sky? Is there a Heaven, a Hell, true love, real hate? Is chaos evil and order good, or is it the other way around? What is the nature of the soul, or is there really a soul? Is it really no thing that can be any thing and every thing? Is my very existence just an error or an anomaly? Is my sentience an evolutionary flaw? What is Art? Do women really desire a large penis? Are we immortal? What, where, how, when? Why? Give up my friends and rejoice! I have been a pillar and a pile of bones, and thousands of lifetimes have I known, and I am no wiser than you are wise. In fact, I don't think I'm wiser than anyone anymore. But I do know that sometimes only a girl in a sundress and the wine she offers can give us any relief from our burden. She will steal it all away, so our flesh dries up, peels off, and tumbles across the desert, becomes dust. We are swept away by the wind and churned with the sand. We become nothing but bleached bone, just as Adam. Sometimes intoxication and an orgasm will have to be enough. And then it is gone. We forget everything we've learned, and must begin again, empty of every thing, even memories.

My bones clattered into a pile on Adam's crypt floor. My skull bounced a few times, jumped up over the edge of his sarcophagus, and landed face to face with his skull.

"Oh Johnny! You're back!" chuckled Adam. "How nice of you to join me like this! This time we can have an intimate chat, skull to skull."

"Hahahaha!" our lower jaws flapped together.

"Hahahahahaha!" we kept flapping, the dust swirling.

Adam looked at me with deep, black eyes and said, "Johnny, the scorpion is going to put you back together and restore your flesh. He will lead you to a cave that will take you into Hades' depths."

"Hades? It's a real place?"

"Call it what you want, but it is where souls go for eternal torment."

"Wait a minute, why would I have to go somewhere for eternal torment? I thought everybody just kept changing forms?"

"You didn't keep changing forms. You failed. You failed the mission I sent you on."

"That's why I have to go to Hades?"

"You didn't change… …did you?"

"Well, no. The snake told me I was the only one who had stopped changing forms, but it was because I had been standing there in the desert, a pillar, for so long. That goddess of the ziggurat compelled me to do it! To stand there a pillar for so many going rounds of the round."

"That's no excuse Johnny. Do you always do what the gods compel you to do? The snake is right. But I must correct you both. You are the last one who hasn't changed forms that is still outside of Hades. There are others like you, but they cannot be among us because they are not changelings. Only changelings stay out of the Pit."

"What? Changelings? Aren't those the very demons you find in Hades?"

"That's not what I meant, bonehead! Words! Words! Call it the place for un-changelings! I don't care! What's a changeling in the other world isn't the same thing as a changeling in this world."

"Well, shit! Are you telling me I have no other choice but to go to Hades?" All because I didn't change fucking forms when it was an innocent mistake? Even though I was following a goddess's guidance?"

"That's right."

"But wait, I was transformed into a pillar! I didn't choose it. I have no ability to turn to stone."

"Then how did it happen?"

"The goddess must have transformed me!"

"Johnny, take responsibility. You did it to yourself. You found the empty pedestal base and stepped up on it. And then you voluntarily turned back to flesh to be with a girl when the time came for a little fun in the sand, right? Jumped right off the ziggurat without a hitch! Don't try to fool me. I've been around a while. You turned into a pillar and just stood there, an un-changeling, while every one else and every thing else made their rounds."

"Cursed to Hades because I chose to be immobile, like stone… …fuck…"

"Now you're catching on."

"But once I'm in Hades, can I ever leave?" This little adventure was becoming quite concerning. Had I been more than bone, I'm fairly certain I'd have felt the terror of the situation tightening my stomach and throat.

"No one has ever left Hades, because, as I said, souls go there for eternal torment. But, from what I hear, anyone can leave. All they have to do is give up their suffering and walk out of the place. But, suffering is what got them there in the first place. Suffering is the refusal to change. No one in Hades wants to change, so they don't want to leave after getting there. That would require a change! You see? Most of us are too possessive of our suffering to ever let go of it, even though Hades is a horrible place, a nonstop torment! There's nothing good about it. Why so many damned souls keep on embracing their changelessness at the cost of so much agony is a mystery to me, so I don't bother asking anymore. I never wanted a taste of any of it. Besides, I'm cursed enough as it is. Lying here nothing but bones, reflecting on my failure, is more than enough to bear."

"So you should be in Hades too! You never changed!"

"Johnny, just shut up! This isn't about me. Now go find your torment and stop trying to blame or think your way through this situation. Logic only gets you so far. Your accusations are pointing into darkness you can't navigate. So, let's focus on the matter at hand. Are you ready to go?"

"Wait, what kind of torment is in Hades?"

"Still asking questions…"

"Just one more…"

"There are 3 kinds of torment in the pit. It depends on whether your vice is idleness, rigidity, or greed. These are the 3 major forms of changelessness. Not wanting to move, not wanting to transform, and refusing to let go of any thing."

Was I really headed for torment, or was this another test? My impulse was to ask more about Hades, how to get out, whether I really had to go, and to explore the vices in greater detail. But I was just going to go along with it, because I remembered Vatsulu's words, and I felt it in my gut:

"Just keep swimming my brother. Go with the currents."

"Bye Adam, I'll telephone from Hell."

"Hahahaha!" flapped Adam, the dust swirling.

One by one, the scorpion picked up my bones and put them in an old canvass sack. He tied it shut, and threw me over his shoulder.

Clank! Clank!

We swam up through the ocean and onto land. We traversed forests, mountain passes, rolling hills, grasslands, and tundra. When we arrived at a place of eternal winter, we stopped. The scorpion untied the sack, dumped my bones into the snow, and went to work arranging them in proper order. He stuck his tail into my eye socket and returned my flesh to me.

"Brrrr! It's cold out here and I have no clothes!" I blurted, as I hopped around in the snow.

The scorpion didn't say a thing. With his pinchers he cut two holes in the canvass sack I'd been transported in and threw it to me. At least I had shorts.

The scorpion pointed behind me, then turned and scurried away.

I looked behind me to discover a small opening in the earth. A cave.

Chapter 9 – Descent into the pit

Hades' gates are not guarded. You won't find Cerberus, a hydra, or a band of skeleton warriors trying to stop you from getting into the place. In fact, there are no obstructions or locked gates to Hades. There are no barriers to entering the Mouth of Hell. You just walk right in. Everyone is welcome, living or dead, though there is only one place where the living may enter, and only a guide can get you there. My guide, as you have seen, was the scorpion. Funny I call him a guide. He was more of a courier. After all, he did throw me into a canvass sack, tie it shut, and carry me a distance before dropping me off at the entryway. I suppose it doesn't matter whether we make it to Hell through a guide or via a courier, or all on our own. What is important is that we make it there.

I pulled the canvass sack up over my legs and girded my loins. Luckily it came with a pull string that served as a belt, once I'd tightened the ends and fashioned them into a bow. Then I took a few breaths, got down on my hands and knees, and crawled into the little hole in the ground which took me straight into a low, rocky and twisting tunnel. There was not enough room to stand, so I had to keep crawling. I was just able to see which direction to clamber into the greater depths, but only because an eerie, gray light glowed from the jagged walls. Soon my knees were raw and it was so cold my teeth were chattering. I couldn't feel my hands, feet, lips, or ears, but I kept going. It seemed I was slowly descending, and I kept going. If I had to guess, I crawled nearly a mile into the earth before finding what appeared to be an end to the tunnel, and there in the ground I discovered a little wooden trapdoor. I bounced on it, tried to pry it open with my fingers, knocked on it to see if someone might open from below. Nothing. Finally, I found a little wire loop sticking out of the stone wall and gave it a pull.

The trapdoor opened!

I dropped straight into nothingness, pure black nothingness. I fell. I fell for a long time. I fell. At first, the horror of plummeting straight into a pit with no apparent bottom made me shut my eyes tightly and yell until all my air was spent. Something about having my stomach thrown into my throat made it impossible to refrain from screaming as loudly as I could, like a little girl, over and over again. At some point I pissed and shit in the canvass sack I was wearing. It was quite a drop. It was quite a dump. I tumbled, and screamed, tumbled and screamed.

Eventually, I realized how ridiculous I was being, so I came to my senses, straightened out, stopped spinning, and opened my eyes.

All around me, what appeared to be souls of the dead were swirling. Midair they were holding their hands out to me, as if in supplication. I had always been afraid of ghosts, but it is amazing how easily you overcome your fear of everything else once you have come to terms with the fact you are freefalling to your death.

"Hey buddy," said a fat man in a panama hat, "do you have anything to eat?"

"I want my daughter back! I was young when I gave her away! Please give her back to me! Please!" cried an old woman.

"He went to prison because I lied! I'm the one who stole the money!" confessed a man in a fancy suit.

"Sorry, I can't help any of you. All I have is piss and shit in my pants, and regrets I just pulled the wrong wire."

The desperate souls made sour faces, turned, and drifted away with hanging heads. I kept falling.

I don't know if I fell for days or weeks, but I had long given up hope of splattering at the bottom when a powerful gust of wind swept me up and began carrying me somewhere. When I looked down, I discovered my body was clasped between the thick, translucent fingers of a monstrous, ethereal hand. After being carried a short distance, a little wooden tavern came into view. It was hovering midair in the abyss, alone amongst the absolute darkness, and a warm fire was glowing through its open windows. The hand flew me to the entrance, the swiveling doors flew open, and I was gently set down on the welcome mat. It said "WELCOME." The hand floated away and I stepped inside.

"God damn! What's that smell?" demanded the bartender. He was standing right there behind the bar. Like the best bartenders, he was a surly man, balding, and had a protruding belly stretching against his greasy, paisley apron.

I looked around to discover I was the only other person in the place.

"Sorry. I shit in my pants."

"What the hell you do that for?"

"I fell into this hole and it scared the shit out of me."

The bartender grinned to his bushy sideburns. "I'd shit too if I fell so far. Tell you what," he pointed a fat finger, "through that door is the washroom. Listen. Go wash up. Rinse out that damn sack you're wearing and hang it by the fire to dry. I have a clean apron for you. I wouldn't leave here with only an apron on though, with your bare ass hanging out for grabs, so stay a while, until your pants dry. As you can imagine, in Hades you won't be a virgin long if you're running around with nothing covering your little brown pucker. In the meantime, come on back and sit on down, have a few drinks to soothe your nerves, get the blood flowing."

I returned wearing the apron, my bare ass showing in the back, the rest of me smelling of lye soap.

"I'd ask you your drink, but here we only serve various devils' brews you ain't never heard of and we can't say the names of them 'cause we ain't got a forked tongue – but I can describe what they do and how they all taste," explained the barkeep.

"What do you recommend?"

"Depends on what you need."

"I need to get out of here."

"There ain't no drink for that."

"Then how do I get out of here?"

"I only know rumors. They say you just have to fall to the bottom, get up, and start walking. There's only one way in and one way out. There's no way to get lost, and no one is going to stop you from leaving this damned hole. Just remember, along the way there will be a lot of places where you'll want to set up camp and stay forever, like at the ale lakes, the shroom fields, or one of the many flesh pits."

"You gotta be kidding me! Ale lakes, shroom fields, and flesh pits?"

"I am kidding," winked the bartender, after a pause. "But there are powerful temptations here, and no one has ever turned his back on all of them, at least that's what I've heard. That's why no one has ever left Hades. It's something about the personalities that fall into this pit in the first place, because everyone is free to leave. But nobody ever has."

"That's what I've heard too. People get stuck here for the same reasons they ended up here. Sounds like I'm in for trouble. Give me your strongest drink, and make it a double!"

As I put down round after round, taking back my warmth and composure, I pondered between pours. And he was a good bartender because he knew I needed the empty silence but a full glass. I must say that though I couldn't pronounce what I was drinking, it was strong and didn't taste bad, like aged whiskey from a foreign land.

What did it mean to find myself falling into a strange place? Maybe it was like being born? Isn't being born like falling into a strange place you've never been before? Living life is like falling into an abyss and you can't see where you're going. Could smashing on the rocks at the bottom be like getting to the end of life and dying? If not death, what is at the bottom? When we are born, we are shitting in our pants as we are falling into it, and throughout life we shit in our pants a time or two, and then when we are old and we know the bottom is close, we shit in our pants a lot. Along the way strange spirits plead to us for things we cannot give them. Other times we run around with our asses hanging out, but here and there we find solace. A gentle hand sweeps us up and carries us to a temporary but safe place. There we clean ourselves and find a fire's warmth, and maybe a friend. Then we must go on. We jump back into the abyss. Once more the darkness swallows us up, and we are falling again.

And so I had my last drink, gave back the apron and pulled my dried shorts back on. I nodded goodbye to the barkeep and he winked back at me. I took a deep breath, walked out the swiveling doors, and jumped back into the pit.

Chapter 10 – A light touchdown

Again I was falling into the blackness, but this time it was because I'd leapt back into it. As I dropped, the spirits of the dead once again came swirling around me, with gloom and despair on their faces.

"Hey buddy, got a cigarette?" asked a bum.

"Sir, can I have a puppy?" inquired a small child.

"Can you show me the way to Toledo?"

"Sorry, can't help you, but do you have a parachute I can borrow?" I teased each of them in reply to their desperate pleadings, and this caused each of them to offer even sadder faces, turn and slowly swirl away.

To kill the time during the long drop, I started doing summersaults and cartwheels. I practiced spinning like a top. Sometimes I sang children's lullabies, and at others I found my body still, my mouth quiet, my mind pondering this and that. What if I'd gone to school to become a chiropractor instead of a lawyer? What if I'd married that accountant girl back when I was 23, had a few kids and a house in the suburbs? What if I'd been a religious man? What if I hadn't lost so many friends over the years, as a result of getting so outrageously drunk at so many parties? Falling into Hades really gave me time to think.

Once I'd tormented myself with enough "what ifs?" and "why did Is?" the darkness began to dissipate and a dim light appeared beneath me. It became brighter and brighter, and blue, until it was as if I were falling into the sky, rather than into the depths of the earth. Fluffy clouds emerged and I fell through them. I dropped straight past birds drifting on feathered wings. Pastel and striped hot air balloons were bobbing about in the distance, as were kites with flapping tails. Then the rooftops of vast suburbs and the greenery of lush parks and the blue waters of lakes came into view below. Shit… At the speed I was going, the ground was coming up so fast I had no doubt I was going to land hard and splatter.

Fear didn't overtake me because the inevitable was so obvious. Instead of fear, I felt acceptance. I wasn't going to survive this fall. Let's just be done with it! I'd finally had enough. I didn't need any more adventure or any more tests. Maybe I should have drowned long ago, when I fell off the bridge? Don't resuscitate me. This was finally too much and I was tired of it all. Hades? This couldn't be Hades. Who cares anyway? I crossed my arms in resignation, let out a sigh and closed my eyes. It had been a good life... I'd seen and done a few things with it, though not nearly enough, but who dies satisfied? All our works are dirty rags, eh? That's from the Bible, isn't it? Oh how we embrace religion when the end is near...

Just as I had offered my resignation and exhaled, from out of nowhere I was snatched up by the elbows, resulting in my stopping abruptly midair. Instead of falling, I was floating. What now? I opened my eyes to take a look, and what I saw immediately lifted my mood. What appeared to be 2 angels had taken hold of me. They were slender, smiling, and beautiful, with feathered wings and bare breasts, and they were wearing diamond-studded g-strings. Each wore a peacock's plume on her head. All right, Adam, I'm game for another test. Just one more! With escorts like these, why not? Oh how quickly a couple pairs of tits can divert us from thoughts of suicide!

The plumed winged girls with bare tits didn't say a thing. They just kept smiling and flapping. Gradually the ground grew nearer. We flew over tract after tract of suburban housing, thousands of little rooftops that all looked the same. A master-planned community stretching to the horizon in every direction, and the only thing breaking the monotony of the dense, checkered patterns were lush green parks and crystal blue lakes. But there was something peculiar about the orderliness of it all. Nothing was unique. That was it. Even the parks and lakes were identical. In each park, children were playing kickball and dogs were chasing Frisbees. In each lake, couples were floating along in kick-paddle boats. The sight of it all gave me the same feeling as listening to a broken record skipping and playing the same beautiful line over and over again, eventually turning it ugly.

One of the plumed winged girls tapped me on the shoulder and pointed. Up ahead, the monotony of the track housing, parks, and lakes broke. We were approaching a small train depot. An old black steam engine was idling next to passenger platform and choking out smoke. When we got closer, I could see a train conductor standing there, waiting. The girls put me down in front of him, giggled to one another, and fluttered away.

"Later girls."

"Welcome to Hades, Johnny."

"You know my name too? I should have guessed."

"I do keep track of all the passengers," he winked.

"This is Hades?"

"Sure is, at least the suburbs of it."

"I thought it was a dark place filled with ghouls and tortured souls."

"Look around you. That's exactly what this place is – a dark place filled with ghouls and tortured souls."

"Then where are the pits of flesh and lakes of ale?"

"My goodness, Johnny, if you are looking to find any of that here, I'm terribly sorry to tell you you've come to the wrong place. You aren't looking for Hades. You're looking for Paradise."

"Let me guess. Your train won't take me there?"

"Nope. Sorry to disappoint you. Do you have any other destination in mind? I just may have a ticket. There are quite a few places to stop along the line."

I scratched my head. Let's see, I thought. Adam said something about vices. The vices must be part of the riddle.

"Where do I go to confront the vices?"

"Vices?"

"Yeah, you know, idleness, rigidity, and greed."

"Oh goodness. Johnny, in Hades, these vices you speak of are not the 3 vices, they are the 3 virtues! And besides, I'm not sure there really are 3 virtues. There may only be 1," winked the conductor.

"Let me guess. Here darkness is light, so vices are virtues? Everything is upside down: 3 may equal 1 and 1 may equal 3? It's one big tangled cluster fuck that's as orderly as can be, neat and tidy here, but anywhere else it would be a mess?"

"Well, not exactly, but close. But don't you worry, my green friend. You have an eternity to seek your answers now."

"I was taught to seek questions, not answers. Don't you know Vatsulu and Adam?"

The train conductor offered a big smile, and his silence told me I wasn't going to get any more out of him. What had he said? I had an eternity to seek my answers? Vatsulu had said to seek questions, not answers… Maybe the trick to escaping Hades had something to do with not seeking answers for eternity? That could be exactly what has kept anyone from ever getting out of the damned place. I had a hunch that was the answer to my escape. Seek questions… don't seek answers…. Easier said than done. The riddle still wasn't solved. How was I to seek questions? Even in asking myself this I knew I was falling into the trap of seeking answers. What was the answer to how I could seek questions and not answers by asking questions? Shit. What is the sound of one hand clapping? I knew asking myself this old Zen question would be enough to help empty my mind, at least enough to get moving, and that was part of it, moving, going with the currents, keep swimming! I knew I wasn't going to get anywhere unless I started going somewhere. Stand in one place and you'll be there forever. An un-changeling. Deserving of a permanent stay in Hades. I'd learned not to become a pillar the hard way.

"Alright, I'll take a ticket. What are my available stops? Do you have a schedule?"

"You don't need one. The train only goes one way, and with one ticket you can get off at any stop. Every stop is different every time, even if it is the same stop you've made before. And whenever and wherever you stop, you can stay as long as you want and then you can get back on the train and keep going, whenever you decide the time is right. When you need the train, go to a train stop and wait. It will come. You'll hear a whistle in the distance."

"What's at the first stop?"

"Like I said, it is always a different place for each person, even if you've stopped there before. It is a one-way ride, but it will take you anywhere you need to go. But most importantly, the final destination, at the very end of the tracks, is the way out, though no one has ever stayed on until the final stop."

Shit. Hades. A one-way street, or should I say train? It is tailor made for each of us, probably to make sure the marginal utility of our pain is maximized with every step we take in the mire. All you have to do is walk out of the place, stay on until the last stop, get off and get out, but no one ever has. Maybe no one ever would, not even me (and for all you know I wrote this damn story from the pits of Hell and I'm still there, still looking for a way out), but fuck it! I'd give escaping a try just to take pride in knowing I did my best to defy Orcus. If there was an Orcus.

I held up a finger. "One ticket. I'm getting the hell out of here."

Chapter 11 – Idling at the first stop

The train chugged along for what seemed many hours. And as it chugged, you just had to look out the windows to see an endless array of tract houses flashing by, flashing past, one after the other after the next. Was Hades nothing but an endless suburb? Who'd have thought? What was I supposed to do here, in a cookie cutter neighborhood with no end?

But there was an end, right? You could just walk out of the place, but no one ever had. You can't get off track because the journey through Hades is one way. Adam's talk of the torment found here – the vices. Or were they virtues instead of vices, as the conductor suggested? What was I supposed to do with them? I wasn't seeking any torment. Or was I? Oh, what the hell. I was in Hades now, and I had to deal with it. I'd done it to myself by falling for a snake. I'd stepped out of permanent stone and into temporal flesh and sand just for a bottle of Chardonnay and a girl in a sundress with no underpants. Come to think of it, that wasn't why I was in Hades. That girl and the wine were only the lure, not the cause of my being there. The sin, or the injustice for which I was suffering, had something to do with my having been a pillar for so long. As a result, I was now an un-changeling because I had just stood there, a pillar in the desert, watching the seasons turn with every slow blink of my eyes. While everything but me changed. I had earned this condemnation. Was I somehow being punished for having taken a taste of immortality that wasn't mine to taste? The tree in the garden is forbidden for a reason, be the tempting fruit a chance to turn to stone, to sip Chardonnay, or to partake of lust with a snake? Partake of the fruit and you just might be in for a ride through Hades' suburbs. Or was it the shrooms, Absinthe, or hashish lollipops? Or the mix thereof? If only I'd never tumbled off the bridge and into the water! Still, I was glad for it. Sometimes you just can't resist seeking the glimmer in the darkness, and that is the beauty of fireflies. They are just little ephemeral specs of hope, flashing randomly in the night, and just watching them blink is certain to tempt you into the blackest places, to go chasing after them.

I was lost in the blackest night, but didn't regret it. Ever since meeting Vatsulu, I'd been on quite an adventure. It was a welcome change of pace from working a dead end, predictable job, from one year to the next, and then one year to the next again. Who else gets escape from it all just once, to swim with a fish bearing a man's face, to be swallowed by a whale and to escape from it by breathing through a mermaid's tit? Not a man sitting at a desk, Monday through Friday. How often do we get the chance to stand as a pillar in the desert for more than a thousand years, take instruction from a talking skeleton, sleep with a snake in a sundress and no panties, or plummet into Hades wearing nothing but a canvas sack? Oh yeah, and the barkeep's whiskey was free of charge. How often are the drinks free in any tavern?

Change and flux. Step into the blackest night after fireflies, my sisters and brothers. Don't just stand there. It is the chaos of it all we must embrace, and if we are worshippers of stagnancy, we will be punished. We are punished for not moving along as we should, for not willingly tasting the serendipity of it all. How we have been and will be all things, so resist it we shouldn't, and just allow ourselves to become dogs, cats, men, women, snakes, and fowl again! And don't forget to seek the questions, not the answers. Chase blindly after the fireflies. They will light the way. Don't catch them or put them in a jar because they must be free to guide you by their glittering pulses, deeper and deeper into the darkness.

Someone was shaking me. "Sir, sir! Wake up! We have arrived at the first stop."

"Er, eh… what?" I'd fallen asleep and the conductor had his hand on my shoulder.

"We've been stopped here for a while, and it's about time to depart. Don't you want to get off at your first stop? Why have you just been sitting here, sleeping when you have so many places to go and see? Your ticket will still be good when you want to board again."

I looked out the window. "It looks like the same place. Haven't we gone anywhere? All the houses and streets still look the same."

"Johnny, it's all a matter of perception. I understand where you are from the sun rises and falls over and over again. The days go from Monday through Sunday, over and over again. Every two weeks you receive a paycheck for sitting at a desk and doing the same thing you did to get the previous paycheck, and the one before that. I hear you have to pay the same bills every month: mortgage, utilities, cable television, water, and trash, even a car payment and insurance! I can't fathom how you can tell one day from the next where you're from. It never changes. I think it is kind of the same thing for you, being a stranger here. Just how you see nothing but sameness in my world, I see nothing but sameness in yours. Everything really is different here, even if to you it all looks the same as everything else, from the outside. It all depends on how you look at it, or maybe it is how you live it."

I scratched my head. "O.k., so if I get off at this stop, and take a look around, I'll start noticing everything isn't the same?"

"Probably not at first," grinned the conductor. "You need to start by looking into things. Not at them."

"Oh, come on, please not another riddle!"

"Try knocking on a door or two."

"Who will answer?"

"It can be anyone you have known that has died. Or hasn't lived."

"Everyone here is dead?"

"Yes. Even if they are still alive back home."

"Even me?"

"Some questions shouldn't be asked, Johnny. Just sought."

"Then this really is the land of the dead?"

"It is Hades."

"And no one has ever left it?"

"Nope. Though there's one way out and there's only one way to get there."

"What about Lazarus? Didn't he come here for a visit and leave after 4 days?"

The train conductor grimaced and his silence spoke clearly. Seek questions as if you are chasing fireflies and not intent on catching them. Don't capture any or put them in jars. Jump from one to the next, from blink to blink, to blink. Get lost in the blackness and you will find your way.

Chapter 12 – Suicide girl

I hopped off the train. When I looked back, the conductor waved goodbye through one of the small square windows. I waved back. The train belched smoke, began pulling its cars up the track, and then chugged away into the greater depths of Hades' tract housing. Still wearing nothing but a canvass sack, I took the stairs off the platform and headed into the suburbs.

Block after block I walked, and still the cramped tract houses all looked the same. It was row after row of continual sameness. At least the blue sky offered my bare back warm sunlight. Block after block I walked, and I just kept walking. Every once in a while I'd turn a corner or cross a street, or look up to see the same front yards and houses. Mostly, I just looked down at the sidewalk and watched my bare feet taking 3 steps on each concrete slab before stepping over a crack and then taking another 3 steps, over and over. There was something to getting into the rhythm of walking, 1,2,3 and 1,2,3 and 1,2,3. With my steps I began saying aloud, "Don't step on a crack or you'll break your mother's back." 3 syllables per slab, 4 slabs each time I said the whole line. Rhythm! That was it! 1,2,3, "Don't step on," 1,2,3, "a crack or," 1,2,3, "you'll break your," 1,2,3, "moth-ers back." 1,2,3,1,2,3,1,2,3... I realized it was Rhythm! 1,2,3,1,2,3... Swim with the currents! Don't seek answers, but find more questions by staying in motion. The stage curtain will open. Your eyes will be filled with light. Finally I blundered. Eventually it will happen. I stepped on a crack and stopped in my tracks. When I looked up from my bare feet, I was standing in front of a familiar house. It was just like the one I'd lived in with my 2nd wife.

It was so familiar I felt as if I'd traveled back in time, as if I were returning home from work like I had so many times before. Maybe I really was? The only indication to the contrary was that I was wearing nothing but a canvass sack, not a suit and polished wing tips as I always had been in the past.

I opened the front door. There was my old denim jacket hanging on the coat rack! It had a Confederate Flag patch on the left elbow. A familiar silver mirror set in a wrought iron frame was hanging on the foyer wall. It had belonged to my grandmother. Stairs lead up to where I knew I'd find her. My body tensed with anxiety. Oh god, I don't want to go through this again… My last encounter with Gina had been a horrible one. The last time I saw her… I could sense I was once again reliving the exact same encounter I had lived over and over again in my dreams and in my memory. But this was the first time it wasn't in a dream or a recollection, at least since it had really happened. I didn't ever want repeat that scene again, but apparently it was too late.

"Johnny! Come on up! I'm in the bathtub!" her voice carried from upstairs. How quickly the sound of her voice put me in a trance and filled me will hope! I was instantly hypnotized. I sighed with relief when I heard her voice. She sounded happy! Could she really be happy? She sounded like she was glad I was home. Had she decided to love me again? All the old feelings of love for her instantly flooded my heart and I suddenly felt light and free again. The trepidation was gone. I had loved her. And in just that instant, I was no longer afraid. I was suddenly madly in love with her again.

"Johnny! Get up here!" she plead.

I darted up the stairs, ran down the hall, into the master bedroom, and through the open bathroom door. There she was, naked in the bathtub, just like she had been the last time I'd seen her. She was sitting in tepid water mixed with dark blood. Her wrists were slashed open, and an open package of razor blades were on the floor beside the tub. I suddenly felt heavy and chained again, cursed with old feelings of grief and guilt. In an instant my feeling of being madly in love again vanished. Pain retook its old, familiar place.

She wasn't smiling, as usual, but this time she was alive. Gina's blue eyes were piercing me with hatred. By her look, I realized she'd feigned her tone of voice to lure me up the stairs, to find her bathing in blood.

"You did this to me!" she accused.

"You cut your own wrists," I spontaneously retorted, and in so doing I was surprised how quickly my old combative attitude returned.

"You were never there for me!" she screamed.

"All you ever did was complain, nag, and bitch!" I yelled back.

"You and all your friends, the drinking, the casino…" she wept.

"I liked being happy, you fucking bitch!" Fucking bitch. I'd said it again. Just like that. How many times had I promised myself I'd never say it again? Those were the words that had replaced her name, Gina, with a new name. Fucking bitch. Not Gina. Fucking bitch. Maybe she had earned the title, but I never liked being required to address her by it. It was her name, not mine. Or was it my name? Anyway, I'd done it again. I couldn't change the way I acted around Gina, or stop using the words, even after her death. Maybe she was partially at fault too. She wouldn't change either.

She sat there in silence, soaking in the tepid, bloody water. I stood there in silence, feeling chained to the floor. The words had been spoken. Fucking bitch. With those words our anger quelled into the stillness of grief. For me for having spoken the words, and for her because she'd been named that name again.

She sniffled and wiped the running mascara from her cheek. "Being happy… That isn't what life is all about. Being happy… Staying away from me because you couldn't stand how I was or how I felt. For you being happy was being irresponsible, refusing to see things the way they really are, and not being able to understand me. If I wouldn't let you *be happy*, you always got angry with me and called me those words…"

"We can all choose to be happy. You just wouldn't ever try. So I gave up…"

And then we jumped straight into the yelling again.

"There were too many problems to be happy! How could you have treated me the way you did, when I was suffering so much?"

"What do you expect? I grew tired of all the bullshit, the depression, the constant therapy sessions, the complaining, nagging, and bitching! God damn it! I could have lived with a year or 2 of it, but you just wouldn't give up being miserable! And your nonstop blaming me for all of it! 2 years turned into 3 and then 4…"

"It was all because of you!"

"I tried and tried. Nothing I ever did was ever good enough. I could never change enough. I never showed enough empathy. I couldn't understand. It was too much!"

"You never listened. You never cared!"

"Like I told you, I couldn't live with the nonstop complaining, nagging, and bitching! The world was nothing but a bad place for you. You wanted me to live in it with you and accept it. Sorry. I couldn't. Sorry. I wouldn't. Sorry. I won't. I'm going to leave you to your own misery, again. There's too much of it for me here. I'm getting back on the train!"

"You aren't going anywhere this time!"

"Why not?"

"We have to talk!"

"About what?"

"Our problems! Why you make me so depressed and miserable! Why you made me kill myself!"

"I don't have any problems, and I never made you do or feel anything!"

"Yes you did! You need to take responsibility!"

"I'm leaving!"

"Just like you did last time?"

"Yes!"

"You can't leave me! You can't leave this place! No one can!"

I turned away, walked down the steps, and out the front door. All the while she was screaming this and that. None of it mattered. Issues. Problems. Incurable unhappiness. The misery I had caused. Everything was my fault. The details didn't matter. I couldn't even remember the details.

As I headed back to the train platform, the guilt and grief over Gina's suicide left me. I no longer felt bad about finding her dead in the bathtub, floating in her own blood mixed with tepid water. I'd done the right thing by just calling 911, giving a statement to the police, packing a suitcase, throwing it in the car and driving away. Though I'd ended up with a foreclosure on my credit report, I didn't care. A mortgage just ties a man down. I'm not sure who took care of Gina's funeral, or if she even had one.

I sat on a bench and waited for the train to come, and I remembered the Gina I'd fallen in love with, the one I'd known before the Gina that had fallen apart. The Gina that wouldn't change.

Before she'd changed into an un-changeling, there was a time we'd hiked deep into a thick forest of Redwood trees. We had a blanket and a basket filled with bread, wine, cheese, and apples. It was chilly beneath the lofty canopy – not at all accommodating for a picnic, but to our joy we discovered a clearing filled with sunlight and warmth. A sunbeam had broken through the arbor ceiling and marked an inviting place on the forest floor. We threw the blanket down, rolled around in one-another's arms, laughed, and got drunk on wine, and naked. While making love we spotted a stag and a doe doing the same thing among the tree-line shadows. They were watching us, and we them, and we were mimicking one-another's erotic motions.

I'll always love the Gina I first met. Somehow she'd died long before I found her body and blood in a bathtub. There was no explanation for it.

Everything in the world had just become too heavy for her. Even happiness.

Some of us give up the journey. Some of us stay a while and get back on the train.

Chapter 13 - The comedy channel

Hades' suburbs. The biggest planned community I'd ever seen. Tract houses in the millions, packed together so closely neighbors could reach out their windows and shake hands. Everyone had the same floor plan. I just sat there, looking out the window, watching it all pass by. My train could have been going in circles, though it seemed we were chugging straight ahead. I'd just keep getting off at each stop and taking a look around. Maybe I'd solve the riddle of how to get out of Hades? Maybe I wouldn't. Seeing Gina again hadn't been pleasant. Somehow she'd managed to win a ticket to suburbia, and I wasn't sure if her suicide was her condemnation's culprit. Adam had said there were 3 torments in Hades, and which one you got depended on whether your vice was idleness, rigidity, or greed. Who knows which one was hers? Maybe she had all of them? She was sitting there in the tub all day, hogging all the bloody bathwater like a pig, being greedy with the razorblades, and being stiff as always, with her bitching and complaining about the same shit over and over again. I could see how all the vices were possibly manifest in her eternal torment. Let her be friends of Brutus, Judas, and Cassius. She could have made a change. Just gotten out of the water and dried off. Taken another path. But that was why she was there in the first place. She didn't want to move, see anything differently, or cling to any hope, let alone let go of her agony, get dressed and go hop on the train.

The train arrived at the next platform. I jumped off. The conductor waved goodbye through a small square window and I waved back, just as we'd done before. Next thing I was back on the sidewalks, counting my steps, 1,2,3,1,2,3, "don't step on a crack…"

When the time felt right, I broke the flow, stepped on a crack, and looked up to find myself standing in front of Larry's old mobile home, an old but familiar sight that had always been there for me during the summers I'd come home from college. Larry was always there and I was always welcome. I knew I could walk in the door any time I wanted, so I didn't knock. I just went right in. The rusty screen door slammed shut behind me. It was dark and cool inside, the blinds were all closed, and a large screen television in the corner of the room was the only source of light. When my eyes adjusted, I could make out Larry's giant form. There he was, all 350lbs of hugeness, reclined and snoring, bare feet up, a padded easy chair serving as his bed.

"Larry?"

"Eh? Snort! Grunt!"

By lunging forward on the springs and kicking at the footrest with his heels, Larry half sat up and looked at me with surprise, but the surprise quickly turned into a gap-toothed smile on his big, round face.

"Johnny!"

"Larry, what the Hell are you doing here?"

"Hell if I know. But before we hug and kiss, go fetch us a cold beer out of the fridge."

I went to the kitchen and came back with two cold ones. Larry didn't get out of his chair to hug me. I bent over and put my arms around his mass while he pounded my back with his thick palms. We cracked our beers and smacked the chilled aluminum together in toast.

"Go grab that folding chair 'gainst the wall and pull it on up!"

I unfolded and pulled the chair up, sat down, and took a big swig. Larry started talking, and he didn't give me a chance to say a thing. It had likely been a long time since he'd had company, so I let him talk. He went on and on about the movies, shows, and standup routines he'd been watching on the comedy channel. I pretended to listen, as I remembered the events surrounding Larry's death. When he was 27, his heart began failing – something about an enlarged heart. When he was 28, he had a heart transplant. When he was 29, his new heart failed and he died. I'd known Larry since grade school and had been one of his pallbearers. He was a good old boy that lived in the country, wore overalls around his big belly, drove a beat up Ford pickup, and he was always filling that truck's rusty bed with empty beer cans. I enjoyed helping with that task whenever I could. As he drove, and we drank, we'd throw the empties out the truck's rear sliding window. They'd usually land in the bed with the other cans, but sometimes they'd jump out onto the highway and roll into a ditch. Larry never worked any job more than a month, and he'd dropped out of high school. Half the time his utilities were shut off. His grandfather had died and had left him with that mobile home and pickup. The only thing that stopped Larry's nonstop talking was the start of a comedy channel sitcom.

"Don't mean to be rude, but I gotta watch this. You'll like it. Go fetch us up round 2."

I didn't find the sitcom funny. It was something about the life and times of some white guy with a big afro.

Larry found it quite funny. Every other line or so, he'd let out a booming laugh.

"Hahaha! Hahaha! Hahaha!"

And he'd laugh some more.

"Hahaha! Hahaha! Hahaha!"

And some more.

"Hahaha! Hahaha! Hahaha!"

It was horrifying. Though we were watching comedy, the whole scene outside the television was something out of Hitchcock, or the Twilight Zone. Whenever commercials came, I went to the refrigerator for more beer, and while I did so I had a chance to ask a few questions.

"Larry, don't you want to get out of here?" I wasn't sure if he knew he was dead, so I said "here" instead of "Hades." I didn't want to be the bearer of bad news, though I had once been one for his corpse.

"Hell no! This is where I live."

"What do you do all day?"

"I don't have to do nothin'. One day I was sittin' here watching my shows and was all bummed out 'bout the empty fridge and out of money, but I got up and looked in it hoping something was in there anyway. And wouldn't cha know it! It was full of food and beer! It has been that way ever since! I ain't goin' nowhere. Ever!"

"Who's been filling the fridge?"

"Hell if I know, but he's a pal of mine. Sometimes I drink all the beer and munch down all the eats, and then I take a nap. When I wake up, the damn place is cleaned up. Not an empty is on the floor where I threw 'em, and the fridge is all full again."

"Don't look a gift horse in the mouth."

"You can say that again! And let me tell you. Since all this good stuff has been happening, I haven't been constipated once and nobody's shut off the water or 'lectric, though I never pay any damn bills!"

"You don't want to go anywhere with me, I take it?"

"Like where?"

"To the train."

"Nobody rides that train. Not after they get off it. I wouldn't get back on if I was you. Besides, I think I'm too fat to fit through the damn door!"

The commercial break ended and the sitcom about the white guy with the afro came back on.

Larry found it quite funny. Every other line or so, he'd let out a booming laugh.

"Hahaha! Hahaha! Hahaha!"

And he'd laugh some more.

"Hahaha! Hahaha! Hahaha!"

And some more.

"Hahaha! Hahaha! Hahaha!"

I stood up and walked out the door without saying a thing. I don't think Larry realized, or cared, that I left without saying goodbye. He had comedy channel sitcoms, beer and food, air conditioning, and never had trouble taking a shit. He was there to stay. Idleness was his virtue. That was easy to surmise. He wasn't changing. No way, no how. Hades wasn't so bad if all you ever needed was free food, beer, utilities, a comfortable easy chair, easy shits, and cable television. For Larry, it was Paradise.

Chapter 14 – Rhonda and the little bull

The train arrived at the next platform. I jumped off. The conductor waved goodbye through a small square window and I waved back, just as we'd done before. Next thing I was back on the sidewalks, counting my steps, 1,2,3,1,2,3, "don't step on a crack…"

When the time felt right, I broke the flow, stepped on a crack, and looked up to find myself in the street, right in front of a large rectangular steel box. It was just sitting there where a cookie cutter house should have been, was about the size of Larry's trailer, and had no windows or doors. A sidewalk led up to it, to right where a front door should have been, but stopped instead at a bare steel wall. However, this strange steel box had a yard, white picket fence, and a mailbox, just like all the other houses on the block. The mailbox had a name on it. "Rhonda." Rhonda? Could it be *the* Rhonda I knew from the other world? Rhonda the painter with the piercings and tattoos? She'd always smelled like lavender and cloves, and I'd never forgotten her. I could swear that last I'd heard she'd been doing great, had married a nice accountant and was painting family portraits from photographs and making top dollar. I had to find out if it was really her, so I went up the sidewalk to the large steel box, to right where the front door should be, and knocked.

"Who is it?" asked a familiar sultry voice.

"Johnny."

"THE Johnny?"

"Yeah, unless you know another one."

"THE Johnny I used to call *my boy*?"

It was Rhonda! "Yeah, that one."

"Come on in! I'm still mad at you though."

"How? There's no door."

"Just walk through the wall."

I felt for an opening and instead of making contact with steel, my fingers disappeared, and then my arm to the elbow, and then the rest of me. I stepped inside.

"Johnny! It is you!" yelled Rhonda, as she jumped on me and wrapped her arms and legs around my torso. I embraced her in return and buried my face in her long black hair. She was naked from the waist down and wearing nothing but a dirty white tank top. I'd always liked how she hated to wear shoes or socks, or panties. I remembered how when we were together, whenever we got back to her place or mine, she'd immediately kick off her shoes and take off her pants or skirt. She smelled like lavender and cloves, just as I'd remembered, and her skin was soft and delicate to the touch, even though the ink that covered it and the piercings which punctured it made her appear much rougher.

"How long has it been?"

"Fifteen years, at least."

"Why did you just graduate and move away without telling me where you went?"

"I don't know. I'm sorry."

"I ended up here shortly after you left."

"But I heard you married an accountant. That you're painting family portraits from pictures."

"How am I doing that? I'm here," she pointed at the floor.

"You have a point," I agreed. There was no point in trying to explain everything now. Besides, I still wasn't sure I even understood anything, especially after having been a pillar for perhaps 1000 years, or 10,000.

"Lay down for me like you used to?" she whispered. "It's been a long time."

"Alright," I agreed.

She let go of me and put her bare feet on the floor. I dropped my shorts and lay down, my back against the cool steel floor.

"My sweet boy," she whispered as she straddled me, pulled off her tank top and draped it across my face. "My sweet boy," she whispered as she slowly enveloped me. As she rocked and clenched I could feel the jaggedness and coldness of her piercings against me, but on the inside she was so warm and delicate. "*My sweet, sweet boy.*" I'm not sure why, but Rhonda could only overcome her sexual anxiety when she was on top and my face was hidden. When we'd started dating, it had taken us at least a month to figure out how to bring her to climax. She'd always been willing to try anything, so one day I'd suggested we turn out the lights, and then she could pretend I wasn't there while she sat on top of me and masturbated, and it worked. As long as she couldn't see my face, I didn't touch her with my hands and stayed beneath her, she could have an orgasm. "I've always said, '*my sweet boy*,' whenever I touched myself," she'd once told me. "Even before we met."

When we were finished, Rhonda climbed off, rolled onto her back and put her feet up high on the wall. "I don't want any of you to drip out. I want your cum in my veins."

"It always felt so good putting it in you."

"Then why did you leave me?"

"I don't know. I was lost. Still am."

"What does that mean?"

"When I get there, I'll let you know."

"You're stuck here now. I can't get out."

"I got in just fine."

"Only one thing ever comes in and goes out. It's this little bull that shows up every once in a while, and I feed it corn," Rhonda pointed across her bare breasts, her feet still in the air. She had black painted toenails and all but her soles were tattooed in paisley patterns, up past her ankles.

Other than me and Rhonda, there were only a few other things inside her steel box, and one of them, which she was pointing out, was a big cloth sack in the corner that read "Yellow Corn Meal – 100 lbs." Otherwise, there was nothing but a three legged stool, a vacant canvass on an easel, and some paints and paintbrushes, and Rhonda, her piercings and her dirty white tank top wadded up in the middle of the floor.

"You feed the little bull corn meal?"

"Yeah."

"Then what?"

"I paint it."

I did a double take of the empty canvass. "You paint it?"

"Yes. When I'm finished painting and the little bull leaves, the canvass goes blank again."

"How many times have you painted the little bull?

"I don't know Johnny, why so many questions? Maybe a thousand times, maybe a million… I don't know."

"And each time it vanishes?"

"What? The bull or the painting?"

"Both of them it sounds."

"Yeah, both of them."

"And eventually the little bull always comes back, you feed it corn meal and paint it, the little bull leaves, and then what you've painted disappears?"

"Yes. That's what I said."

"Why don't you paint something else?" It seemed the obvious question. Painting the little bull wasn't getting her anywhere.

"I don't want to."

"Why?"

"I paint the little bull. That's my job."

"Why?"

"Please Johnny! No more questions. I don't want to have to do anything else. I just don't. Stop asking. Just stop asking!"

"But don't you do anything else?"

"Not really. I masturbate a lot because I don't have you."

"So all you do is finger yourself and paint the little bull?"

"Johnny! Enough! This is my life!" Rhonda insisted. Her feet were still up in the air.

I got up and searched the four walls and the floor, and I jumped up and touched the ceiling in a number of places, by doing so hoping to find a way out. A place to pass through? Or maybe there was a lever or a button? Despite my efforts, I found no apparent way out.

Days passed. Months passed. To pass the time we stared at each other until I was ready to have sex again, and then Rhonda would cover my face and get on top of me, "*my sweet, sweet boy.*" Every now and then, the little bull appeared; Rhonda fed it corn meal from her palms and then painted it on her canvass. Whenever the little bull disappeared through the wall I tried to follow after it, but I always landed hard, face first against steel. And whenever I tried to make an exit, Rhoda tried to stop me, by pulling at me, clinging and shouting, "NO JOHNNY! DON'T GO!"

Perhaps years passed. And then one day it occurred to me. Just a hunch. The little bull always ate the corn meal. That's what allowed him to get out when we couldn't. Eat the corn meal to get out. The little bull always ate it, and he always passed right through the wall, so I would too.

"What are you doing?" Insisted Rhonda. "That's for the little bull! Stop! It's for animals, it might make you sick!"

"I thought it might invigorate me so we can make love more often," I explained, as I choked the dry meal down."

"Oh," her eyes lit up, and next thing you know my face was covered and she was swooning, "*my sweet, sweet boy... ...my sweet, sweet boy...*" When we were finished, I pulled on my canvass sack shorts and tied the ends, and Rhonda put her paisley feet up on the wall. "I don't want any of you to drip out. I want your cum in my veins."

Giving no reply I took 3 big steps and dove right through the invisible front door.

The gods always offer us everything we could ever want, need, or become, and it is usually right under our nose, in this world, other word, now, in the future, or in the past. Just because we can't see it doesn't mean it isn't there. We reject the gods by embracing nothing they offer us, just because it doesn't appear to be there to our senses. We choose obstinacy by refusing to just pass through, to go to the next place, or we don't let anything pass through our nonexistent shells because we are too selfish or stubborn. We'd rather become a stone pillar than go swimming with the flow. Sorry, but we can't just keep painting the same picture time and time again, just because it feels safe. We can't keep painting the same picture time and time again, as all the rest goes round and round, over round, around us. Goodbye Rhonda. We will meet again and next time I'll be on top. Nothing will be lost. My abandoning you is not permanent. Your *sweet, sweet boy* will return, but it may be a while and I may come back as a dog or as a fish, and you may be a mermaid, a scorpion, or a snake.

Chapter 15 – The farmer and his sons, tulips and windmills

I was finally starting to figure things out, not logically, but from my gut. That's where it all starts, you know? In the gut, the deepest part of it. The mind, or the brain, it only rationalizes what we feel, deep in our gut; else it contradicts us and makes us act against our natures. And by gut I don't mean heart. The heart often interferes with the gut's original impulses, and so does the mind. While the mind can rationalize things too much, the heart might give or take too much. But the gut is always right. With Rhonda, the impulse in my gut was to eat the corn meal and get out, which was the right thing to do. But, that impulse went to my heart and my heart told me to stay with her, out of love, and my mind told me to use logic to convince her to eat the corn along with me and to make the escape with me, but both choices were wrong, misguided. Don't ask me why. I'm talking to you from my gut, not from my heart or my mind. The gut compels us but gives no answers.

Just get used to accepting original impulses without follow up or inquiry. Don't be stymied by the heart's regrets or empathy, or the mind's additions and subtractions. It is all abstraction from the visceral reality of things, from your gut. Follow your gut. Only the gut seeks the next question without first demanding an answer to the current question. Go with the currents. Chase fireflies. The heart and mind will get you lost in the desert and you will find the goddess. She will bare her breasts to you, and you shall become a pillar. A scorpion and a girl in a sun dress might show up after 10,000 years or more (and *save* you?). You'll end up in Hades. If only you'd stayed after fireflies…

As I said, I left Rhonda behind, along with that big steel box she called home. I didn't go back to the train platform either. I can't tell you why. I just followed my gut. I walked the other way because sometimes you just must, and I didn't skip or count the cracks. I stepped on every crack, and with every step I broke my mother's back. Rhythm be damned. My gut simply said to go the other way this time and to step on every crack. So I did, without asking *why?* My gut told me the train was a one way ride, and I wasn't headed in any direction any more, let alone in one direction. To be headed in any direction is to know which way or where you should be going before you get there. I didn't know where I was going, or what the next place would be, so I had no direction to know, aim, or go. This made it easy, following my gut. So on my bare feet I walked, and for miles, years, lifetimes, or seasons, I walked. Into the heart of Hades' tract housing I lost myself in the sameness. House after house, park after park, street after street, randomly turning right, then left, going straight, or turning around and going back the way I came again. And this way I finally reached another destination, after 10,000 years or more. As I said, it took miles, years, lifetimes, and seasons, and I won't bore you with the monotony and tediousness of the journey, because it only took time, a lot of it, and time, as we have seen, is a fiction of the mind and the heart. Not the gut.

One day I looked up and discovered I'd finally reached the end of the tract housing. Stretched out before me in every direction were field after field of tulips of every color. Row after row, purple and red, blue and yellow, white and black, orange and pastel and pink, and even many colors I'd never before beheld. Maybe these were the flowers Adam needed? And in the distance, past the fields and still miles away, there were many windmills, tall and four bladed, like stone rooks with 4 swinging arms. At such a distance they appeared the size of thimbles, each standing atop the green foothills that gradually rose from the fields, stretching up and joining to become a single bare mountain capped in snow and hiding its tall peak high in the clouds. It was a mountain I needed to climb, said my gut.

So I crossed the vast tulip fields, ascended the foothills, and began climbing the mountain they became. Up and up, I clambered. Once through the pine forests and into the scrub, I found a little switchback that zigzagged up the rocky face, all the way to the snowline. At the end of the path I began crawling nearly straight up the face of the mountain, my bare hands and feet sinking and slipping in the snow until they were numb and turning blue. Despite my concern I might succumb to hypothermia and frostbite, I kept climbing the best I could, though my muscles were tight and shivering and my teeth were chattering. After all, the only gear I had was a makeshift canvass sack I was wearing as shorts. I kept climbing, nevertheless. And to my good fortune, I finally reached a ledge, pulled my body up over it, and collapsed. Spent of all I had and unable to go another inch, I went completely numb and began losing consciousness. I was certain that the blackness filling my eyes was death.

But of course I didn't die, or I came back from death. How else would I be telling this tale, especially when you are only halfway through it?

When I awoke from my catatonia, I was lying on an old featherbed and covered with patchwork quilts. My canvass sack shorts had been replaced with a full set of old fashioned long johns. I was in someone's bedroom. In it were a dresser with drawers, a steel mirror hanging above it, an armoire, and a nightstand beside my bed. On the nightstand was a full glass of water, waiting for me. Carefully, I sat up and pushed off the quilts, checked my hands and my toes, my limbs. Everything seemed in order and I'd apparently survived any frostbite or injury. To quench my thirst, I seized the glass of water and drank it right down.

With my last gulp, a middle aged man in overalls and a buck toothed smile, heavy work boots, a gloved left hand and a straw hat entered the room.

"There you are lad! Back from the dead!"

"Dead?"

"Figure of speech. Figure of speech. Glad to see you made it. You were out for 2 whole days."

"Thanks for saving me."

"Not a problem. Not a problem. Glad it was you and not one of them!"

"One of them?"

"Yeah, you know, folks trying to get out of Hades. The souls of the dead. My three identical boys and I defend the top of the mountain here because if any of them – those spirits – make it to the very top of it, they return to the other world. So here we sit in this big windmill blocking the little pass that leads straight up to the place where Hades and the other world come together. Come let me show you the ballista turrets! That is if you're ok to walk and all. By the way, my name is Henrietta. Girl's name I know, but it's a long story."

"I'm Johnny."

I followed Henrietta through the main living area, and then outside onto a circular rampart built of solid stone. It overlooked Hades below, the pass leading to the only way out, where the mountain top touched the sky after vanishing into the clouds, down the snowy slopes, the foothills, and the multicolored tulip fields so far below. Henrietta's three identical sons stood ready, each steadfastly focusing his eyes on the pass, each manning a giant repeating ballista mounted on a turret.

"These are my boys, Ishtar, Guido, and Darius. They never let a demon through and never miss a mark."

"When do they come?"

"The demons?"

"Yeah, or is it the spirits?"

"Same thing. No telling when they'll be showing up next. It is always a surprise and you never know how many of them there will be. Sometimes 1000s of them come clambering up the slope right at us! So far we haven't let any of them get past us."

"How did you end up here, defending this place?"

"No telling. I can't remember ever doing anything else."

"What if I wanted out? Would you try to stop me?"

Henrietta looked at me funny, took off his straw hat, and scratched his head with his right hand. "Well, seeing you aren't dead, or a demon, I suppose you could just go on through. We won't shoot you. Besides, you can just go out the back door, follow the pass the rest of the way up the slope, disappear into the clouds, and pop out in the other world. I think you come out in a place called Tulsa, Oklahoma, whatever the heavens that is."

It seemed too easy. There had to be a catch.

"You mean I don't have to go on a quest to find a grail or the missing pieces of a scepter, or anything like that?"

Henrietta scratched his head some more. "Don't think so… …but… wait!" he lit up, and then he began pulling the glove off his left hand. When the glove was off, he held up the remains, an ugly stump missing 4 fingers and a thumb. "You could go get my fingers and my thumb back!" he beamed, generously offering me a hopeful buck toothed smile and bright eyes.

Fuck… why had I asked? Hadn't I learned a thing? Don't ask questions Johnny… Now what was I going to do? Say no, sorry, can't do it, after I'd offered? Just go do it, said my gut. Go get his damn fingers and thumb. Now it was too late to worry about why you volunteered to go on a quest. You were listening to your gut.

I forced a smile and a certain face. "Alright Henrietta. I won't ask how it happened. Just tell me where to find all the pieces."

Henrietta danced about the balcony, but his sons didn't budge. They kept their focus on the pass and didn't relax their grips.

"Follow me!" exclaimed Henrietta. "I'll draw you a map to all the demons you need to visit. Each one has a piece of me. And before you go, you'll need to go pick some flowers, so you'll have super powers when you need them. Like I said, my fingers belong to some very mean characters."

"Great. Which flowers do what? And how do you use them?"

"You just eat the petals. So just pick the petals. I'll write the recipes for all the powers down on the map, right next to the places you'll need to use them – eat them rather. That way you won't risk forgetting when you are under pressure. Always eat your assigned flowers before you run into the demon you are up against, because you might not have time to make a move once you've come face to face with them. And by the way, thanks for doing this. I don't gamble any more. Those missing fingers are a constant reminder that playing dice with demons isn't very smart. They will take everything from you!"

"Starting with fingers," I chuckled.

"Starting with fingers! Henrietta chuckled back, as he held up his deformed stump and waved it around like a prize, making a mockery of it, "and ending with the thumb!"

So, I headed back the way I came, but this time with a mission, down the mountain in search of 4 fingers and a thumb. Henrietta had provided my equipment: matching long johns and overalls, heavy work boots, a straw hat, a red neckerchief, a map to 5 demon lairs, along with a list of tulip petal power recipes hand-written beside each of the lairs, and an empty sack to carry all the petals and fingers I was off to gather up. Down from the snowy slopes, through the pines, over the foothills, and finally into the vast rows of tulips I went. There I filled the empty sack full with fistfuls of petals – petals of every color required by the recipes: red, yellow, blue, white, black, and many more. When finished, I studied the map in preparation for my first encounter. I was as ready as I was ever going to be for fighting Hades' finest.

"Demon #1 Ogre Woman. Go east through the tulip fields until you get to the Creek. Just follow the Creek southeast all the way into the Old Forest and keep going until you get to the Big Cave. The Ogre Woman is in the Big Cave."

And the recipe for dealing with her:

"10 red and 3 blue."

Obviously the red would give me strength for what was going to be a hell of a fight. This was going to be interesting, and it might hurt.

Chapter 16 - Ogre woman

I went east and found the Creek and then followed it southeast. Just as Henrietta had said, it flowed into the Old Forest. After only a few 100 steps beneath the dense canopy of trees, the light faded into darkness, and whenever I turned around to look behind me, I'd catch what seemed to be yellow eyes in the shadows. But in a blink, they'd disappear. Being watched was unsettling, but all I could do was keep following the Creek, as the eyes kept following me. Eventually I found my way to large opening in a steep rocky face, and the Creek flowed straight into its depths. I surmised I'd arrived at the Big Cave, but I wasn't entirely satisfied with the situation, having only two places to go. Stay outside in the Old Forest and risk being eaten by some yellow-eyed beasties, or step inside the Big Cave and meet an ogre that might grind my bones for bread. Why had I offered to go on a quest for Henrietta in the first place? He'd already offered me free passage into the other world. Too late now. I'd followed my gut.

Having no other reasonable choice, I opened my sack and picked out 10 red petals and 3 blue ones, counted them thrice to make sure I had the ingredients right, and clenched them tightly in my fist. I took a deep breath and stepped within a stone's toss of the Big Cave's mouth.

"Hello!" I yelled into the cave.

"Hello?"

After a pause, a gruff but curious female voice replied. "Hello?" it echoed from deep within.

"Hello there," I repeated my greeting, and then I immediately stuffed all the petals into my mouth and began chewing fast. I could be in a life or death brawl at any moment! The taste of the medicine was surprisingly bitter, yet sweet at the same time, but it was no time to be picky about flavors. Just swallow the load.

Gulp!

"What do you want?" the gruff voice questioned, and this time it barely echoed and was much closer than before.

I swallowed hard once more, but this time it was fear. Shit. Why had I volunteered for this? I asked myself again. Too late to reconsider. Think before you act next time. But hell, because I was already in the thick of it and likely couldn't make things worse, I decided to tell her the truth. What did I have to lose? Besides, I was already starting to feel a strange tickle all throughout my body, and it felt like it was warming me to the marrow in my bones. The super power strength must have been kicking in!

I cleared my throat and spoke. "Henrietta sent me. I am on a hero's quest."

"Why? What for? What do you want?" she immediately questioned, and this time she was even nearer, but her voice didn't sound as crusty or rasp.

"I am here for a finger. Henrietta wants it back."

"I don't have a finger. I have a thumb, and you aren't going to get it without a fight! I will kill you and I will eat you!" she warned. "Go away!"

"I am not leaving until I have what I have come for!" I was feeling quite confident. My marrow was feeling even hotter. The medicine was working.

"Have it your way!" She demanded, and then she stepped out of the cave's mouth – out of the shadows. I couldn't believe my eyes! She was a beautiful 7' female creature by any measure, and dripped with unearthly sultriness. She had long white hair and pale blue skin which was smooth and flawless. Her big black eyes hypnotized mine, and then my eyes went on a journey over her delicious curves: her full breasts to her narrowed waist, down over her rounded hips, her long legs to her flawless ankles and toes. A big girl indeed, but she was a goddess — I'd found no monstrous ogre!

When my eyes were finished, I finally replied, "Not if I can eat you first."

"What did you say?" She growled as she began moving my way, her hands held high, with sharp fingernails pointed at me like 10 daggers, as if she were poised to tear me apart.

"I'm sorry dryad, but you don't scare me. You are much too beautiful and delicate to be made of anything dangerous to more than the hearts of men. You are indeed the offspring of this forest's most enchanting magic." Boy were the words flowing from my mouth! I'd all but forgotten about the ogre, though I realized there was a chance it was right behind her, especially if I was being lured into a trick or a trap by this delightful creature. But I wasn't too concerned at that moment, because I was truly enchanted by what was coming straight at me.

Upon hearing my words she stopped in her tracks, dropped her hands, and suspiciously looked down over her body, her long torso and limbs, her full breasts and rounded hips. Then she looked back up at me with narrowed eyes. "Is this some sort of trick?" she nearly whispered.

"Sorry babe, but it isn't. Where I come from you are one sexy dame."

"Where are you from?"

"I am from the other world," I smiled.

She looked down over her body again and then slowly back up at me, and this time her eyes were not narrowed. This time her big black eyes were suddenly timid and watery. "Really? You *really* think I'm beautiful?"

"Sugar, I could eat you like candy."

"You *really, really* mean it?" she plead, making certain of my answer.

I went to her and when my fingertips touched her bare shoulder, she quivered as if she were afraid, or startled, or both. Her breath was soft and shallow, and her flesh was so warm and delicate I felt I was caressing the creamiest butter. As she stood there victim to my hands, her timid shivers began transforming into pleasure-full sighs. I undressed her of her little patchwork garments, letting them fall to her feet, and she smiled shyly as she kicked them away. I removed all of what I was wearing too, and within moments we were locked in a lovers' embrace, enveloping one another as we collapsed to the forest floor. Quickly I was inside her, soaked and engulfed in her heat and tightness. Like this she held me captive in her passionate waters, keeping me tied to her by locking her long legs around me, her clasping hands cupping my buttocks, making them work, refusing to release me until she had swallowed every drop of lust I could offer. Last thing I remembered was passing out atop her swollen breasts which were streaked in my cold sweat, and just as my eyelids were slowly rolling shut, I heard her whisper, "the thumb is yours."

When I awoke, I was alone, lying naked on the forest floor and not far from the entrance to the ogre's cave. The dryad's raggedy clothes were gone, but mine were still there, nicely folded. My boots were shining with fresh polish, and my tulip sack was sitting there on top of one of my boot's toes. I didn't even have to look inside. I knew the thumb was in there. I also knew I couldn't stay. From my headache I felt like I'd awoken with a terrible hangover, and I knew the 10 red and 3 blue tulip petals were both the culprit of my throbbing head and responsible for having done something to alter my perception during the encounter I'd just had. I didn't have to look around to surmise what had happened, but I looked down at the ground, nevertheless, and there were very large, ugly footprints leading back to the cave. They were not the prints of any beautiful forest dryad, even a 7' one. Those red and blue petals had not provided me any physical strength, as I had suspected they would. Instead, they had given me the power to see inner beauty – a beauty that transcends the flesh that is so often holding it hostage to ugliness or the mundane.

At that moment, I realized I'd learned a lesson in one of the virtues. We can't be too rigid with what we see, or we'll never behold beauty beyond what the eyes alone disclose. Sometimes we must see with our hearts and feel with our eyes. If only we didn't have to eat 10 red and 3 blue tulip petals to see what is truly delightful about a sweet girl with a rough exterior.

Chapter 17 – The chess master

I studied the map.

"Demon #2 Chess Master. Go back through the tulips fields west all the way. At the big lake go south and then southwest, staying along the water until reaching Lighthouse. Chess Master is in Lighthouse."

And the recipe for dealing with him:

"10 yellow and 3 purple."

Obviously the yellow would give me enlightenment for the big game. This was going to be interesting.

Once out of the Old Forest, I trod through the tulip fields westward, by keeping the morning sunshine at the task warming my back, by doing so making the assumption that in Hades the sun also rises in the east. Plus the dryad-ogre had been to the east, and now I was just traveling the opposite way. Soon enough, my directions were confirmed when a vast blue lake appeared in the distance, and I could see seagulls hovering above it, taking turns diving for fish. When I was close enough to the lake, I saw the snowy peak of Henrietta's mountain reflecting in the water. Upon arriving at the shore, I turned left and followed the water line south, which after a while curved southwestward. All along the way I made footprints in the sand with my boots. The sound of the gentle waves mixed with the *wack, wack, wack, caaaws,* of the seagulls put me at ease, and it didn't matter how long it took to get to where I was going. I had the sunshine and the seagulls and they were my fireflies. By midday, the Lighthouse appeared in the distance, and eventually the beach turned into a rocky incline leading up to the beacon. At the very end of the climb it became so steep I had to clamber on hands and knees to avoid falling backwards, but I made it to the top, brushed myself off, and ascended a set of spiral stone stairs leading right to the front door.

Clack! Clack! Clack! I worked the brass knocker against the heavy oaken door.

Clack! Clack! Clack!

No one answered, so I waited, and while waiting I realized I'd better be prepared, so I hurried open my pouch, retrieved 10 yellow and 3 purple petals and shoved them in my mouth.

A tiny porthole slid open. "Yes?" announced an ancient voice.

I chewed as fast as I could.

"Who is it?"

I swallowed, *gulp*, and replied, "Johnny."

"Johnny who?"

"Johnny Wraith."

"I don't know anyone by that name."

"You do now."

"You have a point, Johnny Wraith. Now that we are acquainted, why are you here?"

"I don't think *we* are acquainted," I countered. "Only *you* are acquainted. *You* know my name. *I* don't know your name. So *I* am not acquainted." And with that I realized the flowers were taking effect. My powers of logic were clearly enhanced. I once again felt the familiar tingle down my spine that I'd felt right after eating the red and blue flowers at the ogre-dryad's cave.

"Chet Masert. That's me. I keep the lighthouse lit so the ships at sea don't crash upon the shallows."

"What? Chet Masert? I thought you were the Chess Master?"

"Nope, never heard of him. And that's not me."

"And you said this was a sea? Not a lake?"

"Yes. This is the port of Hades. This is a sea if there ever was one, and it is more than a lake. Those are seagulls out there, not lakegulls."

"Wait a minute."

"Alright."

I pulled out the map and looked for a Chet Masert, and there wasn't one on it. There wasn't a sea on the map either; just a lake. Chet Masert? Why did it sound so close to Chess Master? In any event, it didn't matter. I was apparently lost.

"You don't know a Chess Master?"

"Nope. Like I said, I've never heard of him. Why do you ask?"

"Long story, but Henrietta sent me after his fingers and thumb. Seems he lost them in a dice game."

The old voice chuckled through the little porthole. "I've heard of things costing an arm and a leg, but never 4 fingers and a thumb!"

He kept laughing and I joined with him.

"Come on in for some tea, Johnny. You could probably quench your thirst after climbing all the way up here."

A few latches slid and clicked, a chain rustled, and the big door opened up. I stepped inside and found myself looking down into the oldest, wrinkled face I've ever seen. It was toothless and smiling and had a long nose with hair growing out the end. His forehead was big and bald, with zigzagging blue veins bulging from beneath its thin, translucent skin. We shook hands hello, and his hand was soft, loose, and bony in my palm.

"Want a cup of tea?" the old man offered.

"Yes. That would be nice."

I followed him through a narrow corridor and into a little room with a tiny teak wood table and stools. He leaned on the wall to make his way because age and arthritis had nearly immobilized him.

"Sit down, young friend. I just heated it up."

I took my place on a teak wood stool, and Chet set the table before filling my teacup and his with a quavering hand, but not spilling a drop. Then he took his place across from me, on his own stool, lifted his cup to his lips with both his hands trembling, and sipped. I did the same.

"Minty. It's good."

"I grow it myself in the flowerboxes outside. The mint that is. Not the tea. The tea I buy when the good ship Bullwinkle docks here every other April."

"The mint makes the tea."

"I have to agree. I have to agree."

I took another sip, and the old man with the wrinkled face just sat there, as if reading words from my face. When he was finished, he asked me a question I didn't expect.

"What do you want from me?"

What did I want from this old man? I'd wanted him to be the Chess Master, not Chet Masert, and to defeat him in a game of chess so I might win back one of Henrietta's fingers. But that wasn't an option. I was in the wrong place. But I could see from this old man's pleading face that he wanted me to ask him for something. So, I sat there and looked at him in search of what I should desire. Like I said, he had visible, blue zigzagging veins in his forehead. He was ancient and toothless; it was obvious from the way his cheeks and lips sank inward, how the flesh on his face dangled loosely under his chin. He'd been around a while, and with age comes wisdom, they say, so I asked,

"After all the time you've lived and been, what do you think is the most important thing for me to know, as I make the journey from my age to yours? So, what I am asking you to give me is the gift of having a chance at being even wiser than you are now, once I have lived the same number of years."

Chet smiled from ear to ear, showing darkness and gums where his teeth had once been. "Checkmate!" He announced. "That's the game, son, you win! I've never been beaten!" And then he hopped up from the table, hobbled across the floor to the pantry, flung open the doors, and with a quavering hand stretched for a can on a high shelf. "Here it is!" He chuckled. "Old Henrietta's little finger! That was a bad night of dice for the poor fellow! Let me tell you!" And with that, old Chet Masert tossed me the can. I caught it and shook it. It rattled. There was something inside. "Just have to find a can opener," laughed the old man. "I canned it last olive season. Want a can of olives too?"

"No, I'm full. Just ate. But thank you."

And then the tingling effect of the 10 yellow and 3 purple flowers began to dissipate. My vision blurred and I batted my eyes and closed them tightly to refocus. When I opened them again, the teacups and kettle were no longer on the table. A chess board was there, and it appeared my knight and my queen had made the last moves, and put the Chess Master in checkmate.

"See you later Johnny," waved the Chess Master, as I left the lighthouse behind. "Good game!"

"Yeah, good game!" I turned and waived back. "Good game!"

Had those 10 yellow and 3 purple flowers really made me smarter? Wasn't yellow the color of enlightenment? I wasn't sure because I had hallucinated drinking tea, not playing a game of chess. This had to be another lesson in the vices, or should I say virtues? I get the 2 confused now. In any event, I apparently won the game by asking the Chess Master for his wisdom, not by stealing a victory from him. I probably didn't have what it took to defeat him at his own game, to take it from him, but instead, I offered him humility. I generously gave him the curiousness of my youth, at least when compared to his age, and in return he was generous with his ancient wisdom. Greed curses many of us to Hades' flames. You don't just beat the Chess Master at his own game, by snatching it away from him when he's not looking, but he will gladly teach those eager to learn, if they ask for the knowledge with pure intentions. Only this way can all the moves that will win the game against the most experienced sage be properly known and appropriately applied for victory.

Chapter 18 – The juggling clown

I studied the map:

"Demon #3 Juggling Clown. Leave Lighthouse and keep following water's edge with the water on your right side. Keep going through the Swamp and don't stop until you get to a Cobble Stone Road running straight into the water. Get on Cobble Stone Road and go west. Don't stop until you get to the Gorge. The Juggling Clown guards the bridge spanning the Gorge.

And the recipe for dealing with him:

"10 green and 3 white."

Obviously the green would cause me to grow arms or something like that. I couldn't juggle otherwise, with only 2 hands, unless only 1 ball was involved. This was going to be interesting.

I followed the shore south and then west, and then north, keeping the lake on my right, and the grasslands turned to marsh. As instructed, I kept going until arriving at a cobble stone road that ran straight into the water. Following the map, I took the road west, thus venturing straight into the Swamp and the setting sun. The seagulls' *wack, wack, wack, caaaws* were soon replaced by the *ribbit, ribbits* of the frogs of the bogs. The swamp became thicker and thicker, and it mixed with nightfall until I could barely make my way. At times I had to blindly feel ahead with the toe of my boot, so that if I stepped off the cobblestone path, I stopped, took a step back, pivoted a bit, and tried again. Soon the blackness was only lit by the same yellow eyes I'd spotted in the Old Forest. There they were again, lurking, watching, and waiting to leap at my throat? What did they want of me? It was likely not just the satisfaction of their curiosity.

I picked up my pace and with only a few dozen steps, the ever increasing darkness began to dissipate. The light of flickering tiki torches appeared ahead in the distance! I broke into a trot and before I knew it I was in a lit clearing. Here the Cobble Stone Road was lined with flaming tiki torches and it lead straight to a suspension bridge that spanned a vast gorge. A strange character was standing there, on the bridge's wooden abutment, as if he were in charge of collecting tolls. He had an expressionless, white-painted face, and wore a black 3-piece suit. A 3-pronged jester's hat with gold bells at the ends sat on his head. In his hands were 3 silver balls, 2 in the left, 1 in the right. He just stood there, as if my arrival came as no surprise. Realizing this fellow must be the Juggling Clown, I quickly opened my pouch and stuffed 10 green and 3 white petals into my mouth. I chewed fast and swallowed, and then slowly approached him. I stopped just a few steps away from offering him a handshake because he wouldn't return my offered smile.

"Hello," I offered.

"Hello," he replied in monotone.

"You must be the clown?"

"Clown? Do I look like a clown?" he challenged in an agitated tone.

"No, you look more like a politician," I quickly corrected. It seemed the right thing to say, and it made sense. He was wearing a suit, his face was painted, and a jester's hat sat on his head.

At this suggestion, the Juggling Clown smiled ear to ear and stepped forward as if to offer me a handshake, but instead he dropped the 3 silver balls into my hands, 2 in my right, 1 in the left. "A politician, eh? I look like a politician, eh?"

I nodded then looked down at the shiny balls in my hands to discover my contorted face in 3 reflections. Then I looked back up at him, and he was raising his brow as a signal for me to give a more certain reply to his question.

"Yes, a politician," I smiled.

"I always thought my calling was something like that, yes, yes. A politician!" Then he looked down over his suit and dusted his vest with his hands. "Yes, a politician."

The flowers I'd eaten were beginning to take effect because I felt a goose pimple chill come over me, and travel down my spine. The balls in my hands began feeling warmer.

The politician looked back up at me, and his face turned from smiling to serious. "I know who you are, Johnny, and you aren't getting Henrietta's middle finger. I won if fair and square in a game of dice."

There had to be a catch, and I knew it. The dryad-ogre and the Chess Master had given up a finger and thumb, so there had to be a way to get the middle finger from this guy. It couldn't hurt to ask.

"So, even though I got a finger and thumb back from two other players already, you aren't going to give me the middle finger?"

"No. But you can go get it on the other side of the bridge."

"I thought you said I couldn't have it."

"You can't."

"Why?"

"You weigh 1 pound too much to cross the bridge with those 3 balls in your hands. Each ball is 1 pound and the bridge can only withstand 222 pounds."

"How do you know how much I weigh?"

"Besides being a politician, I used to make a living guessing peoples' weights at the circus."

"What do I weigh?"

"200 and 20."

He was right on the money, so I knew I was going to have to play his game. "The middle finger is across the bridge?" I asked.

"Yes."

"I'll just leave the balls here, with you."

"Only the balls will open the door to the shrine where the middle finger is kept, just on the other side of the gorge."

"I'll make two trips."

"Nope. As you cross the bridge, the planks will disintegrate behind you."

"Can I throw the balls across?"

"Nope. It is more than a mile across. You can't throw that far."

"I'll go across naked."

"I wouldn't do that. A horde of horny wing demons might smell your bare ass and come flying out of the chasm for you."

"Look I know this old riddle. I have to juggle across, to make weight, but I can't juggle. That's the problem. This is a riddle for a juggler to solve."

"That's not my problem."

"Then I'll just turn around and go back. Henrietta said I didn't have to return his fingers to get out of here. He should be happy with 2."

"I don't think you can go back the way you came," the politician pointed. I turned around and was startled to see that the yellow eyes were attached to voracious wolves about the size of horses. More than a dozen of them were now standing there just outside the swamp thickets, in the shadows, just beyond the full reach of the tiki torchlight, waiting, licking their lips, watching.

I turned back to the politician. "So, what am I supposed to do? I can't go back. I can't juggle. I'm just stuck here."

"That seems to be the case, Johnny, to you."

"How do you know my name?"

"The Dwarf told me."

"The Dwarf?"

"Yes, he has Henrietta's index finger and he can also be found on the other side of the gorge. He lives beneath the ground. In the Catacombs."

"How did he know my name?"

"The Dwarf? He knows the Queen, and she has the ring finger. The Queen knows everything."

I pulled out my map and the politician was correct. Demon #4 was the Dwarf and #5 was the Queen.

"How do you know who has all the fingers?"

"We were all in the same dice game, obviously."

"So the Queen told the Dwarf I was coming and the Dwarf told you?"

"Yes."

"How did the Queen know I was coming, and what my name was?"

"Like I said, she knows every thing. Let's put it this way. There were really 10 of us in the dice game, because all of us were 2 of us, and one of us was a boy and a girl," the Juggling Clown winked.

Shit. A riddle. 1 of the 5 in the game was a boy and a girl. Let me think. The ogre was a dryad and an ogre woman – both girls, the Juggling Clown a clown and a politician – both boys, the Chess Master also Chet Masert – both boys, the Dwarf I hadn't met but both of him I was guessing were boys. What could be girlish about a dwarf, or queen-like? That was 4, or 8 of the 10, depending on how you looked at it. Then there was the Queen herself… …she made 5, or 10 of the group, and then there was still Henrietta to be counted, which made 6, and 6 doubled was 12! With Henrietta it was 1 or 2 too many in the game. So, either Henrietta or the Dwarf had to be the Queen, but like I said, how could a dwarf be a queen, and how could the Queen have talked to the Dwarf if they were one in the same player? And how could each personality possess a finger if each player only took one? That left only Henrietta wearing the Queen's crown! Shit. That was it. A boy and a girl... A boy and a girl... That was it! Henrietta was a girl's name that belonged to a boy, so he had to be the Queen! The flowers were working after all. Not by offering manual dexterity, but mental dexterity instead.

"Henrietta is the Queen! That's how you all knew I was coming!"

"Johnny, now you are thinking! But that isn't the answer."

"Then it is the Dwarf!"

"Sorry, no more guesses."

"But Henrietta is a girl's name, and everyone else but the Dwarf is either a boy and a boy or a girl and a girl."

The Juggling Clown burst into laughter and he laughed so hard he collapsed to the ground kicking his feet in the air. "You idiot!" he kept laughing and kicking. "Every riddle can't be solved! Not every riddle has an answer! Not every riddle is any thing but nonsense!"

I didn't find any of it funny. But I quickly realized this was his way of teaching me the lesson I'd been failing to learn since Vatsulu first instructed me. Seek questions, not answers...

When the Juggling Clown was finished laughing, he sat up and looked at me, and I asked, "So how am I supposed to get across the bridge?" And just as I'd asked, I realized I'd just asked another question.

"Johnny. Don't think for a change, will you?"

"Give me a hint."

"You have all the time in the world."

So I sat there, pondering. I sat there for days, and the politician just stood there at the bridge, staring into space like a mannequin, with his white face and jester hat with 3 dangling golden bells. And the wolves stayed put the whole time, pacing back and forth, just inside the shadows, licking their chops. For some reason they didn't dare come closer. Was it the light from the tiki torches or the politician?

To amuse myself I started playing with the 3 silver balls. At first I just tossed 1 into the air, back and forth between hands, and then 2 of them, and then 3. After several months I was entertaining myself by juggling the 3 silver balls with ease, then while standing on one leg, and then behind my back, and then in circle 8s over and under my legs as I hopped around, and then… …and then I realized I could juggle my way across the bridge. So that's what I did, and it went without a hitch, even though the planks disintegrated as I walked across them, denying me the chance to return the way I'd come, at least on foot.

"And by the way," the politician yelled to me as I was crossing. "The Queen has yellow eyes!" It was another riddle I'd have to ponder at a later time. Or maybe it was a meaningless riddle deserving no time because it had no answer? Besides, I had juggling on my mind, and by keeping my focus on the 3 silver balls, and nothing else, I made it across. Just as I stepped off the last plank, it disintegrated into sawdust and the entire bridge went tumbling into the abyss.

Once at the other side, I pondered. Had the green flowers really given me anything? Had this 3rd encounter really been a test? Maybe. Maybe not. Sometimes we just have to do something new because there is nothing else to do, and it might pay off in an unexpected way. We can't be idle for idleness's sake. Green symbolizes growth, and that was the color I'd eaten, and my skill set had grown. Now I was a real juggler.

I found myself on a small ledge on the side of a mountain with sheer walls too steep to clamber, so I had only one way to go. Through the mountain via a single passageway – a stone door with 3 holes the size of the balls I'd just juggled across the chasm. After dropping the balls into the holes, the door slid open, stone grinding stone. I ducked my head and stepped into a shrine. It was a small room lit with candles, and right in the middle of it was an altar. On the altar sat a ceramic dish, and in the dish sat a severed middle finger, soaking in anointing oils. I grabbed digit and stuffed it into my pouch.

I stepped out of the shrine and confirmed I was trapped between the chasm I'd crossed, and a sheer rocky mountainside too steep to clamber. There was only one way to go, so I stepped back into the shrine and searched it. Without much trouble I found a little trap door in the floor. I didn't even have to pull out my map to know I'd found the way to the Dwarf. Hades was a one way street, and I knew it. Whether you are taking the train or not, there is only one way to go, and that is straight out, even though Hades throws you a lot of curves.

Chapter 19 – Drinking bout

Before I flipped open the trap door, I took the map out and studied it.

"Demon #3 Drunk Dwarf. Find the trap door in the shrine across the bridge. The Drunk Dwarf is through the trap door."

And the recipe for dealing with him:

"10 dark red and 3 dark blue."

Obviously the dark red would give me alcohol tolerance. What else would a drunken dwarf want to do but drink? The only thing likely to get him to give me his finger was a little contest involving who could handle the most ale. This was going to be interesting.

I opened my pouch and counted out 10 dark red and 3 dark blue petals, shoved them all in my mouth, chewed, and swallowed. Almost instantly I felt the familiar tickle down my spine and suddenly I was thirsty, not for water, but for ale. Down through the trap door I went, into what I soon discovered was a maze of catacombs below, with flickering torches, ghoulish shadows, seeping walls of stone and bone. The bones were from all sorts of hominid creatures, some of them human. Femurs serving as torch handles added quite a gothic touch, as did the stacked skulls, which made up the walls wherever the seeping stone didn't. Toe and finger bones formed inscriptions on the dripping stone in many places. I couldn't read them, but it looked a lot like Latin, or a derivative thereof. Soon I was lost like a rat in this horrific maze and everything looked the same. It seemed like hours before a voice stopped me.

"Hey you!"

"I stopped and looked around."

"Yeah, you! To your left, and slightly up."

I looked to my left and slightly up and discovered a wall of skulls stacked in a spiral pattern, and there was an exceptionally large skull in the middle of the design. Its mandible was flapping, "Just take your next 2 rights and keep going straight. I'm getting tired of hearing your boots going *clomp, clomp, clomp* down the fucking hall."

"Sorry Charlie," just popped out of my mouth, and I suddenly realized I was somehow magically filled with intuition. I knew the voice and the big head, as well as his name, I knew not how, but I knew it. Déjà vu?

"*Charlie?* Did you say *Charlie?*" asked the skull. He sounded perplexed. "I can't believe you just said that! Do I know you?"

"I don't know. I seem to recognize you."

"Just now, *just as you said it* – I just remembered my name! I remembered that Charlie was my name! It was back when I used to be a giant among men. How in the world did you know what my name used to be?"

"Shit, I don't know," I confessed. "I just felt it was your name, from my gut. I mean, that it IS your name," I insisted. I was surprised by my own words. It was as if my body and mind had suddenly become a conduit of enlightenment, of wisdom, or recollection. I simply spoke truth with certainty, without aforethought, and in a spirit of pure knowing, as if I were possessed by something that wasn't me. I was some thing else, but at the same time I was still the no thing me, and the no thing me was manifesting some thing else. Perhaps it was me, but from a different time or place, or one that could have been, or one that one day might be?

"WAS, not IS," corrected the skull, and deep sadness was in his voice.

"Charlie, you are no thing, and so am I. You will forever be no thing. You will also forever be both Charlie and not Charlie."

"I know I am nothing!" wept the giant skull, and large tears flowed from his deep, dark eye sockets.

"That isn't what I mean. Look Charlie. Because you are no thing, just like I am, you have been and shall be every thing too. That's how you can be Charlie and not Charlie, right now. Both at the same time. I was once like you, trapped in stone for a million years or more, but that was when I was a pillar set in the ancient foundation of a great temple with a golden bare-breasted goddess rising above it. A thousand times I watched the seasons change and saw the rain and the wind turn mountains into deserts. And here you are, set in these walls, a skull with no thing but contemplation swirling in the emptiness behind your blackened eyes, the seeping stone serving as your tears. All I can tell you my man is to dream of a pretty girl in a summer dress. She has a bottle of chardonnay in one hand and her hem in the other. She is smiling a seductive smile because she knows you will leap from your stony throes when she lifts her summer dress up and shows you she's not wearing panties."

Charlie's mandible flapped a few times without making a sound, and then he finally inquired, "Does she have small feet and large blue eyes?"

"She sure does Charlie."

"And she has soft skin that has never been touched by a man's sweat, or by trouble, or by sunshine?"

"Like freshly fallen snow."

"When will I have her in my arms?"

"She is in your arms right now Charlie. As soon as you step out of that wall and the scorpion comes and restores your flesh, you will know that she has always been in your arms. Your yearning for her now is what makes having her and touching her so delightful. To yearn for her is as important as possessing her. You must first offer her your empty and desirous heart. Else there will be no place for her to fill when she arrives. You must feel hunger before you have an appetite to satisfy."

"Thank you. Thank you!" cried Charlie. "I don't know what you are saying, but I can feel it in my empty heart that rotted away so long ago! What do I do next?"

"Charlie, don't ask what is next. Accept this empty feeling, remain empty and yearning, and she will come to you. It may take until tomorrow, or another billion years. Just remember that time is an illusion, so it does not matter how many times the clock hands must turn," I offered, and then I turned and began walking away. *Clomp, clomp, clomp!* I didn't make far before Charlie called out: "What is your name?"

I turned and answered, "Vatsulu." It wasn't an intentional lie, and I wasn't sure if it was a lie at all. My gut simply told me to tell him my name was Vatsulu, not Johnny. I didn't ask *why*? I just followed my gut, the next firefly. I went on, made the next 2 right turns and kept going straight. And straight I just kept going, and going, and going, and I kept going. *Clomp, clomp, clomp! Clomp, clomp, clomp!* I counted 10,000 steps, and then another 10,000, and another, and finally I became so tired I shut my eyes and I slept as I walked. Like a zombie down in Hades Catacombs, I just shut my eyes and lead my body forward with outstretched arms and hanging hands; my heavy boots clomping a steady beat. *Clomp, clomp, clomp! Clomp, clomp, clomp!*

I dreamt I was back on the train, once again passing through the suburbs one way. The train conductor was there, just a few cars ahead of me, and he was checking passengers' tickets. One by one, he either tilted his hat to them with a smile, or wrote them up for trying to ride free, or for having paid the wrong fare. I suddenly realized I didn't have a ticket! I had had one at one time, I thought, but somewhere along the way I must have lost it. I could only remember being given one by the conductor, taking it in my hand, and never seeing it again. I checked all my pockets and my pouch, even took off my boots and socks in search of it, desperately trying to find it, though I knew it wasn't there. I'd lost my ticket along the way.

"Sir, please put your shoes back on."

I looked up from my bare feet and outturned pockets, and the train conductor was there, leaning over and smiling down at me.

"Um, I... I..."

"Yes?" interjected the conductor.

I made a worried confession. "I... I... d... don't have my ticket," I stammered. "I... I... lost it."

The conductor smiled from ear to ear. "Dwarves don't need tickets! You little fat guys are always trying to pull one on me!" And with that the conductor winked at me, turned, walked away down the aisle and exited into the next car.

I looked down again at my bare feet and they were short and stout, with hairy little toes. I looked at my hands, and they too were fat with thick, hairy little fingers. I felt my face and discovered a stubby round nose and a long curly beard! Apparently I had turned into a dwarf. Was it the flowers I had eaten, the fact I had taken the trap door into the underground catacombs, or had Charlie turned me into a dwarf with his tears? Or was I still underground and sleepwalking like a zombie, but only having a vivid dream I was a dwarf and riding the train again? And furthermore, what was it all about, my having been possessed with a strange wisdom, as if I were speaking in tongues, haunted of something other than myself when I told Charlie I was Vatsulu? It was too much to contemplate. There were too many questions to ask. I knew the answer, and it wasn't an answer as an answer. Don't seek answers but seek the next question. You can't stop moving. I just had to ride the train to the next stop, get off, and recheck the map for where to go next.

I pulled my socks and my boots back over my fat little feet, fixed my pockets, and checked my pouch. To my surprise, Henrietta's index finger was inside, along with the remaining flower petals, his thumb, middle finger, and little finger. I couldn't remember putting it in the pouch, but I didn't fret over whether I'd lost my memory, or how that finger otherwise ended up with me. I was finally learning to stop dwelling on things, to just accept them without asking *why?* One finger to go. Ring finger.

Chapter 20 – Charming the Queen

I got off at the next stop. As before, I waived goodbye to the conductor, and through the little square windows he waived back at me. The train belched smoke and chugged off.

I unrolled my map and read the notes for obtaining Henrietta's ring finger from the Queen and which flower petals to eat, and was rudely interrupted by several police officers dressed in dark blue. They came running up the platform stairs with pistols drawn.

"Put your hands up or we'll shoot!"

I did as I was told, dropped my map and my pouch, and put my hands up.

"On the ground!"

After having my bearded face smashed into the cement, my hands cuffed behind my back, and taking a few kicks to the ribs and the teeth, I found myself in the back seat of a squad car with lights flashing and sirens blaring. By this point in my adventure, nothing came as a surprise. I just took it as it came. A little blood trickled from my nose and into my mouth and when I tried to spit it out, I lost a front tooth.

"Spit one more time and we'll really knock the hell out of you buddy!" growled an officer through the protective steel mesh that divided the car's front and back seat.

"I'd prefer you knock me out of Hell," I laughed.

"One more word!" threatened the officer.

Just go with the flow. Swim with the currents.

After driving through street after street of track housing, we finally arrived at the parking lot of a large, modern-looking government complex. Large letters on the front of the building read, "COURTHOUSE."

"Let's chain this dwarf up."

Like carrion birds, a dozen of Hades' finest yanked me out of the car, took turns kicking and punching me, and then fit my ankles, wrists, and neck in restraining cuffs. Then they dragged me up the steps and into the COURTHOUSE.

"You will be answering to the Queen for your crimes!"

I laughed through the pain and was answered with batons to my head and knees to the kidneys, but I kept shuffling my chained feet. "Keep up the good work boys!" I sputtered blood over my chin and into my beard.

Down a wide hall we went, my smiling, toothless face now dripping blood all the way down the front of my shirt, my boots dragging the floor. Through wide wooden double doors we went, and into a large courtroom. There in the rows and rows of benches, I saw the faces of many people I'd known in the other world, like Kim, an old high school girlfriend I'd dumped to go out with Nancy. Nancy was on the pill. And there was Leroy, an old roommate I'd left with a big lease payment and the winter's utility bill because I'd just decided to leave town one day, without saying goodbye. I felt like trying out a new town and making new friends. And Jeremy was there too. Back in college I'd stolen his cassette tape collection and taken it to the pawn shop. I needed the money to take Laurie Sue out on a hot date. The list of spectators in the courtroom that day, and the wrongs I had done unto each of them, could have filled an entire book. I was dragged up the aisle, past the audience and the bar, and forced to sit at a table facing an empty judge's platform and podium.

"All rise!"

The room rose to its feet and a baton to the side of my head told me to do the same. Silence befell the room as a tall lanky woman in a white wedding dress, with a concealing veil and long train, entered the room and took her seat at the bench.

"Please be seated."

The room sat. The veiled judge nodded slightly to her right and a nondescript man in a 3-piece suit stepped up before the judge and turned to face the audience.

"Before the court this day is the case of Hades versus Johnny Wraith. Mr. Wraith has been convicted of impersonating a dwarf and shall be summarily executed. Mr. Wraith," the 3-piece suit turned and spoke directly to me, "Would you like to say a few words in your defense before we roll in the guillotine?"

The words "executed" and "guillotine" immediately tightened my stomach and throat and my entire body began to tremble. I had been able to keep it cool through quite a beating, even laugh it off. But the thought of imminent death wasn't as easy to swallow.

"Y… y… yes," I managed to stammer, and then I finally swallowed hard and used all of my strength to stand. Before I spoke I remembered Vatsulu's words. *Just keep swimming my brother. Go with the currents.*' I took a deep breath and regained my composure. "If it pleases the Court, I desire my last meal before I meet my fate. That is all." I was going with my gut, and it said to keep going. And to keep going was to keep following the map, and the notes Henrietta had written on it said to eat 10 pink and 3 white tulip petals before confronting the Queen.

"And what do you desire to eat?" questioned the judge, and from behind her veil her voice sounded soft and familiar.

"I desire to partake of 10 pink and 3 white tulip petals. They are in my pouch."

"And what of your defense?" the judge questioned.

"It is too late for defenses, I'm afraid. I accept my conviction. I did impersonate a dwarf, so I admit my guilt. At this point I only desire my last meal."

"So be it," agreed the Queen, and from behind her veil she nodded to the man in the 3-piece suit. He briefly exited the room through a side door, returned with my pouch and dumped the contents out onto the table before me. The entire room gasped in horror when a severed thumb and 3 fingers fell out, along with a mixture of tulip petals of many colors, and the rolled-up map.

"Don't worry about the fingers," I explained. "They belong to Henrietta, the tulip farmer."

"You stole them?"

"Yes, your honor, and I do believe you have the last finger, the ring finger, and I have come to steal it from you."

Batons came smashing down on me and I fell to the floor.

"Enough!" screamed the judge, as she pounded her gavel. "Order! Order! We will have his head soon enough."

The beating stopped and I cringed in pain as I climbed back to my feet. My chains rattled until I straightened out. Now I was bleeding profusely from my head and face and it was difficult to breathe because many of my ribs had just been cracked.

Go with the currents my brother, I remembered his words, and in the horror and agony of the moment, I was able to find electric currents of joy were there for me, inside my body and sustaining me through it all. There was some thing inside me these fuckers couldn't touch, some thing divine, or holy, and it made the core of my being something they couldn't sully, despite what they did to my body. It was some thing that put me head and shoulders above them only because I had it in me to become some thing else when they were unable to do so. I smiled a bloody smile, turned my head, and spat out my other front tooth. "Can I eat my last meal now?" I asked with a blood-sputtering lisp.

"You may," she answered, and with a single nod toward the table she gave me permission to get into my pouch's spilled contents.

Because my hands were cuffed behind my back, I had to lean over the table to gobble up the 13 petals, 1 at a time as I shuffled through them with my nose to get all the right colors. 10 pink, 3 white. As I chewed my selection, I bled from my face all over the place, the table and the contents from my pouch. With each bite and swallow I tasted my own blood. When I was finished, my chains rattled until I straightened up and stood facing the Queen on her judgment seat. Almost immediately my spine began to tingle, and the sensation not only added to my newfound electric joy, but took away every ounce of fear. I'd just let the words come, from my gut. They still wanted words from me, and I knew it. And they would have words, though I knew my gut would not give them the words they wanted to hear. A man must put his gut first because it is the core of his soul.

"Any last words, Mr. Wraith?"

"Yes, my Queen. As I stand here before you, I confess my guilt and beg that my punishment be quick and severe. As I have been rightfully discovered, I was disguised as a dwarf and in wearing this mask I desired to steal back Henrietta's ring finger from you, your honor. But it was not until you appeared before this court that I realized you are the rightful owner of this finger because it is the ring finger, and you are the bride awaiting holy matrimony. Only when a golden ring is found and placed upon this finger you possess, shall you be able to lift your veil. But sadly, this day will never come. You, though a Queen and Honorable Magistrate, are condemned to remain veiled forever, for it is Hades' command that we each must remain permanently affixed in our own stone. You must remain un-betrothed because you can't rightfully transform from bride to wife. This is why my sin is so great. By becoming a dwarf I defied the law that we do not change. I had my chance when I was a pillar for a million years or more, permanently affixed and immobile, perfectly defined by the purity of my motionless. In this station I was witness to the very changes of the seasons with every blink of my eyes, and before me mountains crumbled into desert. But I chose to leap from my designated station, become a rancorous dwarf, chase after a girl in summer dress, make a mess of Hades, take air from a mermaid's tit, and otherwise disturb the dead in their perfect states of rest, immobility, greed, idleness, and rigidity. For all this, the least I might offer is my head.

From behind her veil the Queen put her hands to her eyes and began sobbing wildly into her palms. Before she collapsed and fell from her judgment seat, she screamed, "OFF WITH HIS HEAD!"

The police seized me, the guillotine rolled in, the crowd went wild, and the next thing I knew I heard a loud THUNK! It was my head hitting the floor, rolling, and spinning in circles. Everything was spinning. I realized it was me, or what was left of me, and I was nothing but a head, rolling down center aisle, between the spectators in their seats. It was all a blur, but here and there I caught glimpses of familiar faces and most were filled with horror. My severed head rolling past their feet was obviously quite a spectacle, and I'm sure my hysterical laughter didn't help matters.

Chapter 21 – Spirit animal

The last thing I remembered, after being decapitated, was rolling down the isle and watching all the faces of my execution's spectators spin past me, while I was laughing all the way. I must have passed out from the shock when I finally thumped into a wall. When I awoke from the ordeal, I was sitting on a shelf, nothing but a head, and looking out into a large, ornate bedroom adorned in jewels, silver and gold, finest silk and lace.

"What did you do?" asked a voice to my left. To my surprise, when I looked over from the corner of my eye, there was another head sitting next to me.

"I was disguised as a dwarf."

"That explains it. I didn't do anything quite as bad as that, but I'm guilty of the same crime."

"What did you do?"

"I took up singing."

"Why is that a crime?"

"Here in Hades, you can't sing or dance, just like how you can't become a dwarf, or anything else."

"Why? How is singing the same crime as becoming a dwarf?"

"Hell, I don't know. The law I was read said something about transformation. That was it. I was found guilty of transformation, just like you were."

"You mean we can't change ourselves or anything about ourselves? Even our voices, with song? How is singing transformational and how is singing and becoming a dwarf the same thing? The same crime?"

"It just is the same thing, buddy… …now hush! I can hear them coming."

The bedchamber door swung open, and the Queen pranced into the room with my familiar pouch in her hands. She was still wearing her wedding dress and veil, and following after her with her long train lifted up in their hairy hands were a dozen satyrs. They had little pointed horns on their heads, cloven feet, and extremely large, erect phalluses that were dripping from their swollen, bulbous heads.

The Queen threw my pouch down onto an ornate night stand and clapped her hands, "Come to mama, my lovelies!" she cried out, and then the satyrs surrounded her and began tearing away her bridal gown, all but the veil. It was quite a horrific scene. Soon there was biting and blood letting and ejaculation in every direction, howling and violent penetrations of every orifice. I couldn't quite see what was happening – it was such a blur of ecstatic and frenetic action – but in the middle of the swarm, one by one the satyrs began falling, or rolling off the large bed and onto the floor, a bloody mess, and dead.

Clunk!

Splat!

The Queen was either snapping their necks or tearing out large chunks of flesh with her teeth. When only one living satyr remained, he was behind her with his hairy back to me, wildly driving his large phallus between the Queens parted buttocks, all while she was face down in a victim, like a feasting hyena devouring his entrails. The last survivor didn't live much longer, for before he spewed the Queen rose up from the corpse she was consuming and howled wildly.

Aaaaarrrrrooooo!

When she turned to make her last kill, I witnessed what was behind the veil. She had a wolf's head and familiar yellow eyes, gaping jaws and rows of bloody teeth! When the last satyr stopped screaming, the Queen collapsed into the mess of blood, bowels and organs, and began snoring. Sans the wolf head and the gore that covered her, she had a nice, curvaceous body.

"You know, we heads are her dessert. When she wakes up, she'll pick one of us for her head pudding," whispered the head to my left.

"Shit," I whispered back.

"Yeah, I'll second that."

As the Queen snored, I just sat there, in my head. Now what do I do? I worried. I guess this is the end. It had been a good ride, my crazy life. I should never have offered to help Henrietta. All this for his damn fingers and his thumb! Besides, he had probably lost them fair and square in that dice game with the devils. Now I was without a body and had only a 50% chance of not becoming the Wolf Queen's head pudding when she arose from her gory slumber.

We sat there for a while in silent suspense, and then my ear started itching. It felt like something was crawling out of it from deep inside my head. The scratching noise was almost unbearable and the tickle of what seemed to be the movement of something through my ear canal, from the inside out, made me grimace and clench my teeth. Finally, the foreign body made it out, sat on my earlobe, and began buzzing. A fly was in my head?

"Johnny," buzzed a familiar voice.

"There's an ugly fat green fly on your ear!" the head next to me whispered with concern.

I recognized the voice. Could it be? Vatsulu?

"Vatsulu?" I whimpered.

"Yes. That's me," Vatsulu replied.

"But I thought I'd never see you again?"

"I never said you wouldn't *hear* me again," he buzzed as he chuckled. "I only said you wouldn't *see* me again, but *you* do see *you* every time you look in the mirror, and if I am correct, a few times you have been me since we were last together. Just a few glances?"

"That's right! In the catacombs! I even said that I was Vatsulu!"

"Now do you get it?"

I used my head to ponder what he was getting at and it popped right into my skull. "Yes! Like you said, we are every thing and no thing! I am you and you are me, and there is no limit to the combination of things we can be! That's why I've been convicted and decapitated! I'm being punished for being a dwarf. In Hades you can't be what ever you want to be, or what ever being offers you to be. You can't swim with the currents! You can't even sing or dance! Even singing is transformational because, as I figure, when we sing we become a singer; we are no longer our static selves. Limiting our selves or others is wrong. That's what Hades is all about. Stagnation and motionlessness. Holding on too tightly to permanence is idle, greedy, and rigid."

"Very good, Johnny! Adam will be impressed, if you ever get out of this predicament and get back to him," buzzed Vatsulu. "You have done well by coming so far. I am very proud of you."

The realization of all that I'd learned, and Vatsulu's affirmations of my progress, put a smile on my face. It was sweet, but bittersweet, because getting to this point had taken the sacrifice of everything but my head and I'd even lost my two front teeth. "Thanks for every thing you crazy fish, dog, and fly!" I offered with a toothless lisp.

"You already said thanks," buzzed the fly. "Now listen. Time is short. Maybe it is time for you to be me again? I hate to break it to you, but there is still more for you to come to understand. Ever since we first met, you have been talking to your self. I have been the manifestation of all the things you can be or have been, or could have been in alternate realities. You have come back to your self, through me, from different places and realities, the future, and from history, all in order to be your own guide."

"Alright, I'm not surprised there's still more to learn. But I've certainly learned that at times like these there is no time to look for more answers.

I wish we had more time to hang out and chat, but the imminent danger of my becoming head pudding is paramount. Now get back in my ear old buddy. I need all my wits to get out of this one!"

So I got back inside my head and devised my escape. I was Vatsulu, and I was Johnny, so I obviously had the talent for shifting shapes because Vatsulu was quite a shape shifter. But what shape to take? Wings would be helpful, so I imagined myself flying through the air. Without a hitch the feathers of a dove sprouted from my ears! I outstretched my wings and hit the head beside me in the face.

"Hey! Watch it buddy! What are you doing?"

I began flapping, and soon I was hovering in the air, a head with wings. I was Vatsulu. I was Johnny with wings!

"Hey! Get back here!" yelled the head. "I don't want to be the pudding!"

"Grow your own wings, mother fucker! It is up to you whether to stay the same or to change. Try singing!" I offered, and then I began flying about the room, looking for a way out and trying to figure how to snatch up my pouch on the night stand and make my escape.

The head on the shelf kept yelling, and his noise soon stirred the Wolf Queen from her slumber. When she saw me, she started lunging and snapping at me, as I dodged and dove in the air. Seeking safety, I flew into a high corner and hovered there as the Wolf Queen kept leaping and lunging for me, only falling slightly short of getting her hands and snapping teeth on me. Think fast! Think fast! I had to get the pouch and get out of there. Then I realized my spirit animal for the day. I was like a crab because I was often a little bit slow and clumsy, but I was resilient and had a heck of a hard shell. So, I sprouted legs and pinchers from my severed neck and made a sudden dive for my pouch. The Wolf Queen lunged and snapped at me, and only managed to bite off one of my back legs.

"Ouch!"

Aaaaarrrrrooooo!

With the pouch in my pinchers, out a side window I flew, and soon I was high over Hades' vast suburbs, track housing that stretched into infinity. When I was certain the coast was clear, I landed on a random rooftop, recaptured my breath, and checked the contents of the pouch. All 4 fingers and the thumb were in there, but the map and tulip petals were gone. Mission accomplished! It was time to get back to Henrietta and get the hell out of this place. I'd had enough. However, I knew I had one more thing to do. I needed to pick flowers. Flowers for Adam. Then I had to grind his bones into ashes and dust.

With a pouch filled with 4 fingers and a thumb in my pinchers, I took off for Henrietta's snow capped mountain. As I flew over the vast expanse of tract housing, I couldn't help but remember my friends and companions, Larry, Gina, and Rhonda. Even in Hades I had once again abandoned them, and now my gut was telling me to return to them yet again. Could I save them? I didn't know. My gut was speaking. Should I go see Larry again? The answer was yes. My gut said I should. No more questions. Leave the mind out of it. Just go. Swim with the currents. But first, Henrietta.

Henrietta was delighted to see me, and I told him the whole story of my adventure. "I can't believe I have all my fingers back, and my thumb!" he cried with delight as he hugged the pouch to his chest. "For this I owe you more than gratitude! Seeing you are nothing but a winged head with missing teeth and a crab's body minus a leg, I am forever indebted to you. I can't believe the Queen beheaded you! How awful! But now I understand her a little bit better because now I know she is a yellow-eyed wolf behind that veil. Now what to do about you? Maybe we can build a scarecrow body and you can be its head? You would be a great lookout, a help to me and my sons. You are welcome here."

"Don't worry about me," I assured Henrietta, and before his eyes I flew up into the air, sucked in my wings and crab pinchers and legs, popped my body back out of my neck, and lightly touched down on the floor before him. "On my journey, I have learned that I am not only Johnny, but at different times and places, or even right now, I am also Vatsulu."

Henrietta just stood there staring at me, wide-eyed and slowly nodding in half-understanding.

"Mind if I pick some flowers?" I asked.

Henrietta shook his head. I sprouted angel's wings, and took off into the air. The 10-fingered farmer and his triplet sons waved goodbye to me from the parapet, and I waved back from the air. I suppose it took a visitation from an angel to finally distract those 3 boys from their work.

After visiting the fields and with flowers in my arms, I flew in search of Larry, Gina, and Rhonda.

Chapter 22 – Flowers for Larry

I found Larry's trailer without much trouble. It was easy to find my way because nothing was looking the same anymore; everything was becoming familiar to me, right before my eyes, as if Hades itself were suddenly merging together with the other world I had once known. From the air the streets began slowly shifting and transforming, until appearing to be the same ones I'd walked and driven before I'd fallen off the bridge and into the water. Each park was now familiar to me, not a replica of all the others as they had been when I'd first arrived. I flew over Lake Elizabeth and recognized the wide paved sidewalks around the water. I used to walk my dog Betsy there. I spotted Memorial Park and its Olympic size swimming pool, and its large oak trees and the merry-go-rounds and the old fire truck with the bell you could ring. The houses were no longer indistinguishable, cookie cutter tracts. Each one was suddenly more familiar to me, more so each time I blinked my eyes.

There, down below, was the grey shingled roof and double chimneys of my boyhood home! And there was grandpa's little house with the big back yard, its surrounding chain link fence, and the 40' pine tree he called Bruce the Blue Spruce! Suddenly everything was now known to me, and each house was unique, and I knew everyone in each of them. While I recognized everything, I knew it wasn't an exact replica of the world I had known. Instead, it was an exact replica of everything I had specifically known in the world I'd come from, a microcosm of it, so that only the people and places I knew were included and nothing was foreign. Additionally, all the places and people I knew from all the periods of my life were now merged into the present. Nearly 40 years of neighborhoods had become one big current neighborhood. For instance, grandpa's house, which I'd known as a small boy, was next door to the house of my current boss, Larry. In other words, this new world was constructed from all the different places I had been, past and present.

Everything I'd ever known now existed in the same place, at the same time.

Because I'd learned of the fiction of time and place, I now knew Hades as I knew the other world, and there was no distinction between them. I no longer needed to escape any thing or to find any thing. I knew everything was in flux and should I return to the other world, I might find all that was previously familiar to me changed into cookie cutter houses and unfamiliar streets, foreign places and strange people. All I really needed to do was swim with the currents. As I became any thing or every thing, or drifted about between forms, places, and times, I would cycle through it all as long as I didn't stagnate, become stone, or insist that I'd found any immutable answer to anything. I had finally arrived at knowing how to fly, just as I had learned to swim, and flying and swimming were the same form of motion. Both means of travel, wing or fin, or even train, would get you to where you were headed as long as you didn't insist on knowing your destination, solving any riddle, or reconciling a thing. I was chasing fireflies without trying to catch them. Just going from one to the next and not putting them in jars.

Flowers in one hand, I sucked in my angel's wings and knocked on the familiar, flimsy trailer door.

Knock, knock, knock!

"Come on in, you son of a bitch! You know you ain't gotta knock!"

I stepped into the cool darkness, and it was familiar and inviting. I missed how being with Larry always felt like being at home to me. Just being with him always made me feel like I had a place to be; and I could always come and go as I wanted.

"Fetch us a couple cold ones and get the fuck on over here. There's an empty easy chair here for ya now. "

I put the flowers down on the counter and went to the fridge. Then I found my chair, plopped right down into the overstuffing, worked the lever on the side, and put my feet up. We cracked our beers, slapped them together in toast, aluminum on aluminum, and took big swallows.

"Ahhhhh!"

"God damn, Johnny! You just up and left without a good bye, and you missed a couple good shows. There was even a new guy doing stand up and he was fat like me. He was talkin' 'bout how when he took a shit it was so big his pants fit looser when he was done wiping his ass! Anyway, I'm glad you are back."

"I might not stay."

"You never did stay. What's important is that you always came back. You never knew when 'cause you always got snatched away by college or new twat, but once school was over or the bitch got to be too much fer ya, there you was a knockin'!"

"Yeah, Larry, you've always been here for me and I've just shown up whenever I wanted and took it for granted you'd always take me back like not a day had passed."

"That's what friends er fer, me man! If we did it any other way, we'd be enemies or something else that wadn't as good."

"I know that now. It took me goin' to hell and back to figure that out, but now I know you always have to go back to where you started, and you can't fret it."

"Yep, go with the flow me brother."

"Swim with the currents."

Again we smacked our beers together and took big swigs.

"You like the padded recliner I gotcha?"

"Yeah, you went out of your way to put it in here for me?"

"No, I just woke up after a nap the other day and there it was, a sittin' there, ready fer ya to put your ass on down in it. But it's fer you all right. No question 'bout it."

"Pretty comfy."

"Yep. And just so you know, I finally saw one of them gremlins that cleans up the place and fills up the fridge. All I gotta do is clap my hands and this little fella – I call him Fido – jumps out of the shadows, and I say something like 'BEER!' and he goes and fetches one fer me. I tell ya Johnny. Shit just keeps getting better and better. One of these days I'm gonna have to find a bedpan so when I need a piss or shit I'll just have Fido slide it under me."

"Bedpan!" I exclaimed, and we laughed at that. Then we finished our beers, crushed the cans in our palms, and threw them across the floor.

Larry clapped 3 times:

Clap, clap, clap!

A little gremlin leapt out of the shadows, and Larry placed his order:

"Fido! 2 Beers!"

Fido brought the beers, we cracked them open, clunked cold frosty aluminum on aluminum in toast, and had a long swallow.

Larry aimed the remote and turned on the television, and I stayed for a while. I'm not sure how long I stayed, a few days, a week, a month, or a year, but I wasn't keeping track of the time anymore. We drank beer, we watched old comedy movies, told old stories, drank beer, took naps, laughed, and had a good ole time.

"Fido, Beer!"

"Hahaha! Hahaha! Hahaha!"

And we'd laugh some more.

"Hahaha! Hahaha! Hahaha!"

And some more.

"Hahaha! Hahaha! Hahaha!"

"Fido, Beer!"

Then one day I stood up and walked out the door without saying a thing, and I took the flowers I'd left on the counter. I don't think Larry realized, or cared, that I left without saying goodbye. He had comedy channel sitcoms, beer and food, air conditioning, and never had trouble taking a shit. He was there to stay. For him it was Paradise, and he deserved it. Idleness was his virtue, and maybe it wasn't a vice. Besides, he wasn't changing. No way, no how. Hades wasn't so bad if all you ever needed was free food, beer, utilities, a comfortable easy chair, easy shits, and cable television. I'd be back, and there was nothing wrong with that. I was always welcome at Larry's place and could come and go, or stay, as long as I wanted. I even had my own easy chair there. Larry didn't fly like I did, but I wasn't certain he wasn't flying in his own way, or that I was any different than Larry. After all, for both of us, Hades had become our own personal realities. Larry wasn't seeking any answers, or reconciliations, or trying to solve any riddles, and now I wasn't either. Who needs answers?

Fido, Beer!

"Hahaha! Hahaha! Hahaha!"

And he'd laugh some more.

"Hahaha! Hahaha! Hahaha!"

And some more.

"Hahaha! Hahaha! Hahaha!"

Fido, Beer!

My angel's wings popped out of my back, I flapped a few times and took off into the air, flowers in hand. Maybe bathtub Gina, my second wife, could use them.

Chapter 23 – Flowers for Bathtub Gina

Flowers in hand, I landed in the street in front of that old familiar house where Gina and I had lived, back when I was an aspiring trial attorney. It was the only house I'd ever owned, two stories, brick, with fake Roman columns. Actually, I never owned that house. The bank owned it and I paid a large monthly mortgage for the *privilege* of living there. It was home, and it wasn't. It had that old familiar feeling, but it wasn't the same feeling I had when I was at Larry's place. It had been a good place to take a nap on Saturday afternoons, because I'd had a very comfortable $4000 mattress in that house, and the street was quiet on weekends because there weren't ever any young kids playing in that neighborhood. Young parents rarely have the money to live in the upscale places. Also, Gina was always gone on Saturday afternoons. It was about the only time she ever left that house, to go knit and take tea with an 87 year-old lady a few doors down.

I sucked in my angel's wings, took a deep breath, and exhaled. Before I made it to the front door, I stopped and remembered what I used to be wearing when I came home at 6:12pm every evening, and instantly I was dressed in it: a dark blue suit, a solid yellow tie, black polished wing tips, and briefcase in my left hand. In my right hand I held the flowers. I stepped up to reach for the door handle, but my hands were full, so I sat the flowers down beside the doormat – "WELCOME!" – straightened up, and tried to open the door. It was locked. Then I remembered my keys, so I reached into my pocket, found the master key on the ring, and let myself inside.

In the foyer, I found old, familiar things. There was my raggedy denim jacket hanging on the coat rack! It had a Confederate Flag patch on the left elbow. The familiar silver mirror set in a wrought iron frame was hanging on the wall. It had belonged to my grandmother and was engraved with ivy patterns. And the stairs just to my left lead up to where I knew I'd find her. But this time my body didn't tense with anxiety over how I knew I would find her upstairs. I knew she was up there, lying naked in the bathtub with her wrists sliced open, her entire body soaking in her own blood. I'd lived this exact encounter a million times in my dreams, memories, reality, imagination, or whatever you want to call it. Déjà vu? And I knew I would be here again and again, and would forever be returning to it. But this time, for the first time, it didn't affect me, hurt me, or bother me. I felt nothing but a mild sense of happiness and ease, a new kind of lightness of being. I stood there at the bottom of the stairs, and waited for her to call for me. *Johnny! Come on up! I'm in the bathtub!*

"Johnny! Come on up! I'm in the bathtub!" her voice carried from upstairs.

The enthusiastic sound of her voice no longer entranced me, or filled me with hope that this time it would be different. It wouldn't be different. She sounded happy, but I knew she couldn't really be happy. She sounded like she was glad I was home, but it wasn't really the case. This time I didn't hold on to the vacant anticipation that she'd turned around and had decided to love me again. I knew all the old feelings of love we'd once shared would never return. She could not change. She could not love me. I could love her, but only in another time and place: I could remember what we'd once had and embrace it, even return to it time and time again in the past or in the future, but not here, not in this house, not in this place, not at this time. Here, in this house, she would forever be soaking in the bathtub, in a bubble bath of her own blood. This time I was no longer afraid, but neither was I any longer in love with her, in this particular situation.

"Johnny! Get up here!" she plead.

I slowly walked up the stairs, down the hall, into the master bedroom, and through the open bathroom door. There she was, naked in the bathtub, just like she had been the last time I'd seen her. She was sitting in tepid water mixed with dark blood. Her wrists were slashed open, and an open package of razor blades were on the floor beside the tub. But this time, seeing her no longer made me feel heavy and chained, cursed with old feelings of grief and guilt, or anger. My lightness of being remained.

She wasn't smiling, as usual, and this time she was alive rather than dead. In the other world, the first time I'd found her like this, she had been dead, but in my dreams and in Hades she was always still alive. Gina's blue eyes were piercing me with hatred. By her look, it was obvious she'd feigned her tone of voice when she lured me up the stairs, to find her bathing in her own blood.

"You did this to me!" she accused.

I offered her a tender smile, sat my briefcase down and took a seat on the edge of the bathtub. "Yes, you are right, and I am so sorry."

"You were never there for me!" she screamed into my face.

I cupped her icy shoulder and she flinched, but my continued contact started relaxing her rigid flesh. Slowly the warmth began returning to her, and I felt my blood flowing into her veins. "I know."

"You and all your friends, the drinking, the casino..." she softly wept.

"I know, and I was so misguided. I can't fathom how I behaved the way I did when you were here at home, waiting for me, and needing nothing more than my coming home from work to embrace you. Now, when it is too late, I realize what I needed was always here. Here at home. I threw it all away. I was a fool. I am so sorry baby."

She sat there in silence, soaking in the tepid, bloody water, her eyes wet with sadness. I sat there in silence, not letting go of her, flowing into her with my warmth, filling her empty veins with my living blood.

She sniffled and wiped the running mascara from her cheek. "All you ever wanted was to 'Be Happy!' That's what you always said, you fucking son of a bitch! That isn't what life is about! Being fucking happy! All you ever did was avoid me because you couldn't stand how I was or how I felt. You just couldn't deal with me because I'm a real human being, with feelings! For you *being happy* was always about being irresponsible, refusing to see things the way they really are, and not being able to understand me. If I wouldn't let you *be happy*, you always got angry with me and called me those words... So many times, you called me those horrible names! Fucking bitch! Fucking cunt! Well, fuck you! Fuck YOU, Johnny! Look at what you've done to me, you fucking asshole, you god damned SON OF A BITCH!"

Her flesh began losing its warmth again, and the blood I had poured into her began flowing profusely from the gashes in her wrists. I let go and stood up.

"Baby, I know... I know. Give me a minute and I'll be right back. I promise I'll be right back. I left something I brought home for you outside."

Gina huffed and crossed her arms over her bare breasts, and the blood continued flowing down over her stomach and into the tepid water, darkening it more.

I went down the stairs, out the front door, and shut it. I turned to the door, stepped up onto the "WELCOME" mat, and then I stepped backward, out of my old body, leaving my old self there and only taking the Vatsulu part with me. The old me was now wearing the dark suit and yellow tie, and I was back in nothing but a canvass sack which served as my makeshift shorts.

"Go ahead and go inside," I told myself.

He turned to me and looked at me funny, as if I were an annoyance.

"Who are you? And what are you selling? Where are your clothes?"

"Johnny, I am Vatsulu, and to you I look like a naked man, but in truth I am a Boston Terrier, a fish, a fly, and even more. One day we shall meet again, in Amsterdam."

He turned to me squarely and raised his fist. "Look mother fucker! I have enough problems of my own, without having to deal with the likes of you. Now get the fuck out of here before I kill you!"

I bowed to my old self, turned, and walked away. I waited until I was down the street, out of sight, before sprouting my wings and taking off into the air. I had come a long way. Returning to myself and seeing the rage and pain I had once embraced made me realize just how far I had come, and my newfound humility let me accept that one day I would return to what I had been, requiring me to journey to Amsterdam once again, to partake of Absinthe and shrooms. I would forever return with forgetfulness, and repeat all the same mistakes, but that was ok because it is all part of the going with the flow. The currents will carry us upon their soft boughs, if only we will let go. Leap into the darkness to chase the fireflies, but do not catch them. Don't put them in jars.

As I flew away, the guilt and grief over Gina's suicide left me. I no longer felt bad about finding her dead in the bathtub, floating in her own blood mixed with tepid water. Maybe I hadn't done the right thing by just calling 911, giving a statement to the police, packing a suitcase, throwing it in the car and driving away. I'm still not sure who took care of Gina's funeral, or if she even had one.

As I flew above it all, I remembered the Gina I'd fallen in love with, the one I'd known before the Gina that had fallen apart, the Gina that wouldn't change.

Before she'd changed into an un-changeling, there was a time we'd hiked deep into a thick forest of Redwood trees. We had a blanket and a basket filled with bread, wine, cheese, and apples. It was chilly beneath the lofty canopy – not at all accommodating for a picnic, but to our joy we discovered a clearing filled with sunlight and warmth. A sunbeam had broken through the arbor ceiling and marked an inviting place on the forest floor. We threw the blanket down, rolled around in one-another's arms, laughed, got drunk on wine, and naked. While making love we spotted a stag and a doe doing the same amongst the tree-line shadows. They were watching us, and we them, and we were mimicking one-another's erotic motions.

I'll always love the Gina I first met. Somehow she'd died long before I found her body and blood in a bathtub. Perhaps I was partially to blame, but then again, maybe I wasn't. There was no explanation for it because sometimes you just have to let go. Cut off a part of you and leave it there, but don't leave all of you standing there as a pillar forever. Otherwise, the world will just become too heavy and happiness will no longer be possible.

Some of us give up the journey. Some of us stay a while and get back on the train, and some of us eventually learn how to fly. Don't worry, for even once we have learned how to take to the skies, we will always fall from it with broken wings again. There on the ground we will forget how we once soared high above it all in the heavens, and then we must once again begin that long journey on foot, with complete amnesia. But do not fret. As long as we do not stop trudging forward into the unknown, we will once again be flying high above it all, caught up in the loving embrace of the astral plane's deep blue sea.

Chapter 24 – Flowers for Rhonda

On angel's wings I flew out past the tract housing, Chet Masert's Lighthouse, the lake, the swamp, the politician and his collapsed suspension bridge – I waived down to him but he was too busy juggling for the yellow-eyed wolves to notice me up in the air – the chasm, and into the shrine. Through the trap door and into the catacombs I went.

"Hey Charlie!" I echoed down into the weeping bone tunnels.

"Charlie!"

"Charlie?"

Finally a voice called back. "Vatsulu?"

When I found the big skull he was just sitting there smiling, in his own head.

"Aren't you going to ask what took me so long?"

"No, I'm still dreaming of the girl with the bottle of wine and the sundress with no panties."

"Is she doing cartwheels?"

"Yes, and high kicks!"

"Charlie, I think you've got it. That's why I'm going to take you to her now. She isn't wearing a sundress, but she is the very girl and will be able to restore your flesh."

Charlie smiled even bigger. He was all teeth because there were no gums or lips on him. I smiled back up at him, while thinking of a way to dislodge the big head.

A hopeful but yearning look came over him. "Why are you doing this for me Vatsulu?"

"To free me from myself. I was once you. And you must free her because you were once a part of her."

"You were once me?" Charlie intoned confusion.

"Yes, like you I was once a giant among men, but now I am something else."

Charlie chuckled. "Vatsulu, you and all your riddles! You may not be a giant, but you sure are an angel!"

Angel, that was it! I had wings! So I flapped up into the air, wrapped my arms around the big old skull, and pulled and pushed with all I had, even flapping my wings for lift. Uhhhhgggggggghhhhhh! Heave! Ho! And with a mighty pull and flap, Charlie dislodged. I flew through the air, bounced off the adjacent wall, and landed flat on the ground. The impact knocked Charlie from my grip and he went rolling down the hall. Luckily, no one was hurt. I dusted us off and picked him up, and with his navigation we got out of the catacombs. Soon we were flying through the air. "Weeeeee!" yelled Charlie.

On our way to Rhonda's, I realized we'd forgotten the flowers, so we touched down at one of the parks along the way and found a rosebush. Charlie chose 13 roses he liked the best and I picked them as he pointed them out, "no, not that one," and "yeah, that one," and so on. When 13 long stems were between his teeth, we took to the air once more. With a few hundred flaps and glides, we were touching down in front of Rhonda's house, that big rectangular box with no windows or doors. A sidewalk led up to it from the street, to right where the front door should be, but it stopped at bare steel. Though her house was quite different than the rest of the houses in the neighborhood, like the rest of them she had a white picket fence and a mailbox, and a green well-manicured lawn. The mailbox had the right name on it. "Rhonda."

"Rhonda... Rhonda, good old Rhonda," I whispered aloud. This was the last place in Hades that still wasn't familiar to me.

Charlie heard me, but he couldn't talk because he had 13 long stems clenched between his teeth.

"Mmmmmppphhh?" he muttered.

I knew what to do. It just came to me as if I'd always known it. It wasn't through logic or by logic I was guided, or even my heart. I just acted from my gut and didn't question it. My gut whispered to me and I listened, and acted.

"Charlie, the girl in this house is going to paint the flesh back on you. I've spoken her name, and it is Rhonda. She is a painter and her body is covered in tattoos and piercings. She smells like lavender mixed with cloves and when you are once again a goliath, you will carry her to safety and you will buy her a summer dress and a bottle of Chardonnay."

"Mmmmmppphhh?" muttered Charlie and I didn't answer him. Instead I sucked in my wings, lifted the big skull up and put it on my head like a helmet, fitted so I was looking out his eye sockets. "Let me do the talking my friend, don't say a word." I took the flowers out of his mouth, fixed them into a nice bouquet, and knocked.

"Who is it?" asked a familiar, sultry voice.

"Charlie."

"THE Charlie?"

"Yeah, unless you know another one."

"THE Charlie I used to call *my boy*?"

"Yeah, that one."

"Come on in! I'm still mad at you though."

We stepped right through the steel wall.

"Charlie! It is you!" screamed Rhonda as she snatched up the flowers, jumped off the floor, and wrapped her arms and legs around us. We embraced her in return and buried our face in her long black hair. She was naked from the waist down, wearing nothing but a dirty white tank top splotched with paint. We'd always liked how she hated to wear shoes or socks, or panties. We remembered how when we were together, whenever we got back to her place or ours, she'd immediately kick off her shoes and take off her pants or skirt. She smelled like lavender and cloves, just as we'd remembered, and her skin was soft and delicate to the touch, even though the ink that covered it and the piercings which punctured it made her appear much rougher.

"How long has it been?"

"Sixteen years, at least."

"Why did you just quit your job and move away without telling me where you went?"

"I don't know. I'm sorry."

"I ended up here shortly after you left."

"But I heard you married an accountant. That you're painting family portraits from pictures."

"How am I doing that? I'm here."

"You have a point," We agreed.

"Lay down for me like you used to?" she whispered. "It's been a long time."

"No," I have a better idea. I'll sit on that 3-legged stool over there and you'll paint me."

She let go of us and put her bare feet on the floor. She looked at the stool, and then back at us, while scratching her head. "Well, um, ok… If you don't want to be my *sweet boy* and make love… I guess I can paint you. Is it me? You don't think I'm sexy any more?"

"No. You are plenty sexy, but right now you have to paint us. You just must. You have to trust us."

"Us?"

"I mean me."

"Um… ok… but I only have one canvass and I can only use it for the little bull."

"That's not a problem. I want you to paint me. I mean I want you to paint my body. My skin will be your canvass."

Rhonda smiled at the idea. "That sounds awesome! I tell you what. I'll do it, but I get to paint whatever I want!"

"You have a deal."

We sat on the stool and Rhonda mixed her paints. With easel and brush she got to work on us, and each cool, wet stroke was a pleasure to our skin.

"*My sweet boy*," she whispered, as she outlined a mermaid on our left shoulder. "*My sweet boy*," she cooed, as she drew a scorpion on our back. With her free hand she balanced against us, so she could lean in close to focus on the tiny details of her strokes, and her touch was warm and delicate. "*My sweet, sweet boy*," she whispered, and because the breath from her lips was so near, the softness of her words caressed us.

When she was finished, our entire body was painted from toe to nose, and Rhonda made us stand up so she could make several rounds around us, making sure not a detail of our journey had been left out. Even Henrietta and his triplet sons had a place on our right thigh.

"Don't move," she advised. "I don't want any of you to drip or smear. Let it all dry."

"We aren't in a hurry."

"You always used to be in a hurry."

"Not any more."

"Are you going to be in a hurry to leave me this time?"

"No. We will never again part. I was lost, but now I'm not."

She smiled an uncertain smile, but there was no doubt she was happy with the idea Charlie was never going to leave her.

"Well, Charlie, if you are going to stay, there's one thing I need to warn you about. It's this little bull that shows up every once in a while, and I feed it corn," Rhonda pointed across the room to a corner, to a big bulging cloth sack that read "Yellow Corn Meal – 100lbs."

"You feed the little bull corn meal?" asked Charlie, as I stepped backward out of his new body.

"Yeah."

"Then what?"

"I paint it."

"You paint the little bull?"

"Yes. But when I'm finished painting and the little bull leaves, the canvass goes blank again."

"Oh, I thought you painted on the bull, like you just painted on my skin."

"Now that's an idea!" said Rhonda. "We'll have to try that when he shows up next time."

"That sounds like fun!" said Charlie.

"Charle?" Rhonda changed the subject.

"Yes?" replied Charlie with endearment in his voice.

"Lay down for me like you used to?" she whispered. "It's been a long time."

As Charlie started moving to the floor with a big grin on his face, I tiptoed out of the big steel box, popped out my angel's wings, and leapt into the air. When I looked back from above, the big steel box was no longer there. Rhonda's old apartment complex had taken its place.

The gods always offer us everything we could ever want, need, or become, and it is usually right under our nose, in this world, the other world, now, in the future, or in the past. We reject the gods by embracing nothing, or by seizing a single thing and not letting go, by refusing to let any thing and everything freely flow through our nonexistent shells, by becoming a pillar, or not swimming with the currents. We can't keep painting the same picture time and time again, because we must paint every picture from every scene, time and time again, as we go round and round, over round. Goodbye Rhonda, and hello again. Nothing is lost, and this time, though I have abandoned you yet again, I have given you a part of my body to keep forever. I have given you Charlie, a giant among men. Your *sweet, sweet boy* no longer needs to return to you, for though he is forever lost, he is always with you. Now he is a giant among men, but he may come again as a dog or a fish, and you may be a mermaid, a scorpion, or a snake, or a goddess, or a skeleton, or Vatsulu, or a fly, or an ant. He may be a firefly, so never put him in a jar.

Chapter 25 – Swimming with the currents

I took to the air and didn't look down. Below me was every thing, Hades, the other world, all my memories of this life and all others I'd lived, the lives I'd live again, and the lives I'd live in the future, over and over again. A beautiful chaotic swirl entranced in frenzy. Only from its ever-changing entirety could the single answer to the only question be granted, but only as long as it was never sought by the mind or the heart. Only my viscera, my gut could ever pray to this great loving mother and be heard, and she would give the single answer to me only as a random impulse, and the single answer would never be the same. To sin against her love and wisdom was to challenge her promptings by seeking permanence or certainty, by demanding answers rather than swimming after question after question into the blackness, but never getting too close to her blessed flashing beacons, her fireflies.

I soared high into the emptiness, the pure essence of no thing offered in the highest astral plane. Straight up I climbed until the other world disappeared and the paint on my skin and the canvass sack I was wearing disintegrated, leaving me naked of all things and every thing. I did summersaults and dips, and dives in the absolute darkness, until through motion alone I completely transcended all but the absolute frolic and pure laughter that emanated from my gut and echoed into the void. And only then did she appear, not with fins or a tail this time, but as a red-haired girl with a bottle of chardonnay in one hand and the hem of her summer dress in the other. When she lifted the hem to show me she was wearing no panties, "Hello Vatssssulu," I took her into my embrace and as a bright comet we went spinning across the astral plane, and the radiating light we made left behind a shimmering stream. From this blazing tail newborn stars spun off and took their places in the heavens. Each was a blinking firefly.

Chapter 26 – Farewell Adam

I had returned home from Amsterdam, though I never went back to it after tumbling off the bridge and into the water. After all, the other world and Hades, or this world, or that one, had all melded into one, so there was no longer any difference between one place or the other for me. It was all only one place, though it was every place. I live in this world now, so I live in your world, right now, even though to you it may seem we are in entirely different places. Yet, the proof of my existence is that you are reading my words, and the proof of your existence is that you know, down deep, that you are me, and that I am you. Not only am I Vatsulu, but so are you too.

For old times' sake, the red haired girl transformed back into the mermaid, and in her embrace she took me from the greatest heights back down into the depths of the ocean, while I sucked air from her breast. I needed to visit Adam.

"Johnny!" flapped Adam's mandible, and the dust began to swirl up from his sarcophagus.

"Adam!"

"So lad, I must say this is quite a surprise. Why have you already returned to see me so soon? I thought I'd sent you on a quest so you could bring me flowers, grind my bones to ashes and dust, and go scatter it all about."

It hit me like a shovel to the face. I didn't have to ask any questions. I already knew that, and here I was learning it again. My gut told me I wasn't even close to starting Adam's quest. Besides, I'd forgotten the flowers.

"I just missed you, Adam."

"Well, you aren't doing away with me yet," swirled the dust. "Besides, where are my damn flowers?"

I just smiled and nodded, and listened.

"Now listen up you idiot!" insisted Adam. "Every word I speak causes more of me to crumble away because my bones are so damn old. And by the way, you have figured out that you are going to grind my bones to ashes and dust just by listening to me, right? That's right – you aren't going to be finished with your journey until I have yapped myself away into nothingness, turned into ashes and dust through my own vibrations, by giving you instructions. So, for once, are you ready to listen up?"

"Yes."

"Ok. Henrietta, you need to knock off this Johnny and Vatsulu bullshit for a while. Now listen: first, you need to take my left femur and go find someone that can carve it into dice…"

Made in the USA
Coppell, TX
10 November 2021